A Wolf In Women's Clothing

Wendi Bear

Published by Also I Hate Donuts

Copyright © 2019 Wendi Bear

ISBN: 978-0-9888997-7-3

DEDICATION

I dedicate this book to my daughter and everyone who has the strength to come out as their true self. Stay strong and brave and keep on doing you. Always remember, haters are a good thing, they exist because they are intimidated by your personal power.

You are beautiful!

CONTENTS

ACKNOWLEDGMENTS

A big thank you to Craig Yarger for yet again, cleaning up my terrible grammar. Shelly Cohen Dunlap for reading my filth and giving me feedback when it was still a messy draft. Deva Bales for encouraging me to keep writing this crap. Last but not least, Rachel Hammon for inspiring me to create this piece of utter garbage.

You all rock!

I merged onto a busy expressway. Traffic was heavy and moving at top speed. I traveled ten miles and was approaching my exit when I saw him.

Between the express lanes sat a young cotton-tail rabbit. He had planted himself between the two yellow lines separating the lanes. Each passing car created a harsh wind that blew his ears back and forth. His eyes looked intense as he planned his next move.

"How did he get there?" I wondered, "How would he escape?" The rabbit needed my help, and I had to save him. I considered pulling over, but if I did how would I get to him from in between five lanes of cars? Even if I made it that far without getting hit myself, he would run into traffic to get away from an approaching human, after all he was a wild animal. Perhaps a call to animal control? A police car running its lights would stop traffic. But I knew they wouldn't help a wild rabbit and even if they did, by the time they arrived it would already be too late.

I realized I lacked the power to change his situation. He wasn't my responsibility. I wished him luck and continued my drive.

I couldn't save the rabbit.

INTRODUCTION

It all started two summers ago on a muggy mid-June evening. "Put on your nice button-down shirt, Franklin," I instructed my nine-year-old son. "And for the love of God, brush your teeth. They are orange!"

Franklin gave me the "death stare" before heading into his room to adhere to my demands. I opened my closet and pulled out a black dress I was hoping to squeeze my overly curvy rump into. Lately I preferred a few glasses of wine and a bag of Cheetos over my nightly run and it was showing. I hoped a pair of control top pantyhose would help, but after stuffing my beer belly into them, I didn't think I had much hope. Honestly, I was just praying the seams around my derriere wouldn't rip out. I grabbed a small bottle of clear nail polish for good measure and secured it into the side pocket of my purse.

"Franklin!" I shouted.

"I'm right here mommy!"

His tiny voice startled me and I jumped. I put my hand over my chest, "Oh honey, don't sneak up on me like that." I was recently diagnosed with high blood pressure and rapid pulse. The last thing I needed was an adrenaline kick to send my heart into atrial fibrillation.

"Sorry."

"It's all right, let's go."

Tonight I would expose my spawn to the wonderful world of art. The two of us loaded into my tiny, outdated car. It was a short drive, only about fifteen miles into the neighboring city. After we drove the coastal highway, I located an empty spot on the street with a view of the Pacific Ocean. Once parked, we headed inside and did a beeline to a narrow bar in the far corner of the room. I ordered myself a tall glass of rosé along with a miniature bottle of water for Franklin. We both took sips from our refreshments as we made our way across the gallery floor.

The first exhibit was a collection of old black and white photographs of ancient automobiles. "Check out that one, Franklin. That's how cars used to look a hundred years ago!" I said, trying to drum up interest in my little dude. After all, boys were supposed to love cars, right? "It's called a 'Model T'." He wasn't having any of it. Franklin took a quick glance at the photo but was more interested in a group of children playing on a bench in the center of the room.

"Come on Franklin. Let's see what's on the other side of this wall." My son followed as I made my way to view pieces from the next artist. Once again I tried to gain his attention to no avail. An echo of laughter flooded the spacious building. We both watched as a group of kids around Franklin's age bounded down a small set of stairs leading to a lower level exhibit.

"I want to go down there!" Franklin said.

Happy that my kid was interested in something, I obliged. Following the laughter, we inched our way down the tiny staircase and within seconds, Franklin saw it.

I watched him cautiously approach the painting, as if he was floating to it. He reminded me of one of those old cartoons where the character smells something delicious and is dragged by his nose to the pie. Only in this case the pie was a nude portrait of a large-breasted woman.

Or was it?

I realized why there had been so much laughter from the children. This wasn't a regular nude painting you would expect to have seen from Michelangelo or another "one of the greats." Nope. This model had a little something extra...

That's right, she had a penis.

Noting my son's obvious obsession over this controversial centerpiece, I inched him a bit away from it. "Stand here," I urged, while pointing to a small table facing the artwork from a few feet behind. I left him there to gawk and went back to the bar for another glass of wine. I needed something to take the edge off.

A few minutes later, I returned to the table. Franklin hadn't moved a muscle. "Wow, you are into this painting, aren't you?" He nodded his head without batting an eye.

"Why do you like it so much?" I asked.

"I didn't know girls could have penises."

Pondering his reaction for a few moments, I asked him, "Do you want to be a girl?"

The question led him to break his gaze. He turned and looked me straight in the eyes, "Yes."

Unsure of how to respond to his confession, I spat out, "Well, what should your name be?"

Franklin searched the table and spotted my glass of pink wine. "Rosé, I mean Rosie."

There was no looking back. That night, on our way home from the art show, I took a detour to our local Target and let Rosie pick out a female wardrobe.

She's been Rosie ever since.

CHAPTER 1

"This is your fault, you know. You are a sick human being, Asterisk, to do this to your child. Everyone knows you are forcing Franklin to be a girl. You need psychiatric help."

I glanced away from my phone screen toward a clock on the wall. It looked ancient. Forty-eight minutes had passed since I entered the waiting room of the LGBT (lesbian, gay, bisexual and transgender) Center. Glancing back to my Android, I gave the text message from Rosie's father, the middle finger.

Rosie had been attending therapy the last several months without her dad's "permission." Today the counselor informed us that Rosie couldn't pursue her treatment without her father's written consent. He didn't live near and was seldom in the picture.

It wasn't going well.

With a creak, the old rust-hinged door to the waiting room opened. I watched as my child and her counselor, Ms. Jess, walked out.

"Rosie did well today!" Jess told me. "Children who come out at such a young age are lucky, especially when they have the support of their families. It's very important. We find that some older kids enjoy dressing up as the opposite sex when they hit middle and high school. They think it's 'cool' but it can end up being just a phase. When it occurs at younger ages, it's mostly permanent. I can't even express how delighted I am that Rosie has your support. The suicide rate is statistically greater in transgender youths compared to cisgender. But the rates drop dramatically when these youngsters have access to treatments such as hormone therapy. In California, the state views 'bottom surgery' as a lifesaving necessity."

"I wasn't aware of that," I said.

"Yes! Medi-Cal will cover sex reassignment surgery for transgender youths ages 18 to 21!"

That dumb bitch might as well have thrown a brick at my face. Yes, I would support my child through her physical transformation but I was not ready to hear about my tween having her penis cut off!

"Well, Rosie will have to decide when she has matured. I'm not prepared to be liable for that one!" I said.

Jess chuckled. I didn't see the humor.

"Here's the consent form for the dad. Maybe you want to leave his phone number? Sometimes when a counselor calls direct, they ease up." Jess gave me a wink. "See you next time, Rosie!"

Summer ended, and it was time for Rosie to go back to school. In preparation, we met with the principal, the school counselor and Rosie's 4th grade teacher-to-be. We discussed important changes such as making sure everyone used Rosie's new name and the correct pronouns (she/her/hers). We also discussed which bathrooms Rosie would use (the ladies), and if she should be introduced to her class as transgender.

Rosie had the school counselor accompany her the first day of school to explain her transformation. We had a plan in place to prevent bullying. Things could not have gone any smoother. Rosie started her first day of school as female. She was as excited as Nemo was to start his first day!

Most of her classmates accepted her new persona. Although, one horrid little monster named Jade set out to destroy my daughter.

"You aren't a real girl! You can't be in here!" she taunted Rosie as she attempted to use the girl's restroom. In class, Jade called Rosie by her old name and pronoun. "His name is not Rosie!" she projected to whoever would listen, "It's really Franklin!" Rosie's teacher, in his last year before retirement and unwilling to rock the boat, sat idly by and ignored the ongoing abuse.

Because of the constant harassment, Rosie stopped using the bathroom altogether. Instead, she held it in for the entire school day, eventually soiling her panties. Repeatedly, I picked her up after school and before she told me, I'd smell it.

I called the school and met with the principal again, who promised to protect Rosie from her bully. When that wasn't effective, I emailed complaints, and spoke with other teachers and parents regarding the situation. The harassment escalated. Halfway through the school year I received a call from the principal.

"Hello, Ms. Five," she greeted me. "This is Mrs. White, Rosie's principal. I am calling to let you know I suspended Rosie from school for one week because of inappropriate behavior."

"Excuse me?" My shoulders slumped. "What happened?"

"There was an incident in the restroom today. A group of four girls were all playing nicely together at recess. Rosie wanted to join them. Being a tight-knit group of friends, they told her 'no.' Because they did not give Rosie permission to play with them, she became angered and chased them. Although we don't support 'cliques' in our school, we also don't allow chasing and following others. We consider that harassment."

"Uh-huh."

"Rosie's four classmates ran into the bathroom to hide and she followed them. She stretched her arms and legs across the exit to prevent them from leaving. Once trapped, she instructed them to pull down their pants and underwear so she could see if they were 'real' girls."

My heart stopped. "Oh wow, that is terrible. However, I have a hard time believing it occurred, Mrs. White. Rosie will not set foot in the girl's restroom and hasn't for months because of Jade. She holds her bowels and bladder all day long and has been having accidents in her pants just to avoid the harassment. I have sent you more than one email referencing this exact issue, all of which you have ignored."

"Although Jade was involved..."

I wasn't finished, "If Jade was the ring leader then this would be the perfect example of bullying, wouldn't it? Isn't this what you promised to help prevent in the beginning of the school year?" I felt my blood boil as I tried to keep my cool. "Ms. Five, each child was brought into my office individually and asked for their version of the incident. All four girls said the same thing, Rosie trapped them in the bathroom. I asked Rosie if they were lying, she said 'no.'"

"Rosie doesn't do well under pressure! She thought you were trying to get her to 'name call'. The school needs to be taking care of these issues before they escalate! Jade seems to exhibit psychopathic tendencies, don't you agree?"

"You need to calm down, Ms. Five. Rosie starts her suspension immediately. I hope you talk to your child about 'what is' and 'what is not' acceptable behavior for school."

I slammed my phone onto the counter.

When I picked Rosie up from school, I noticed her face was pink and puffy. "What happened today, honey?"

Tears streamed down my little angel's face. "Am I in trouble?"

"They suspended you from school, but you are not in trouble with me."

"I was playing tag at recess and chasing Manuel. There was a group of girls hanging out near us. Jade was one of them and she was whispering a secret to the others. Two of the girls came up to us and asked me if I 'liked' Manuel. I said 'yes' because he is my friend. Then everyone laughed."

"Honey, when someone asks you if you 'like' someone that means they are asking if you want that person to be your boyfriend or girlfriend."

I watched Rosie's face turn red. "I didn't know," she whispered.

"Then what happened?" I asked.

"Manuel got upset that everyone was being mean, and he left. I didn't want to stop playing, so I chased the girls instead."

"Then what happened?" I pressed.

"They all ran into the bathroom."

"And you followed them in there?"

"No, Mrs. Becky, the playground teacher, saw me following them and took me into the office. I got in trouble for chasing."

"That's not why you were suspended. It's because the girls said you locked them in the bathroom and told them to pull down their pants."

Poor little Rosie's face looked like she had eaten a ghost pepper. It was clammy and puffy with clear fluids draining from every orifice.

"Don't worry Rosie. I know that Jade is a lying brat. You enjoy your time off from school. I'll take care of her," I promised.

CHAPTER 2

"**W**here's Joey?" Rosie asked, peering out of the car window. We were in the parking lot of a grocery store waiting to meet up with Rosie's best friend and his grandmother. For as long as I could remember, Rosie spent at least one weekend a month with her disabled friend and his family.

Joey had a severe case of autism and was prone to "meltdowns" and the occasional seizure. He had been our neighbor for years, until his parents moved the immediate family out of the city. Joey spent weekends with his grandmother who was still local. Joey's grandmother enjoyed having Rosie over because her grandson found my child's calm nature soothing. Other parents shunned the boy, scared that his erratic behavior might rub off on their own kids. Rosie had the magic touch.

"There they are!" My daughter pointed to a large green van traveling in our direction. It pulled up next to us and stopped. We watched as Joey's grandmother opened the driver's side door and slid out, heading in our direction. Joey usually jumped out and ran to greet Rosie.

"Who do you have with you today?" Joey's grandmother asked, peering through my car window. "Is it Franklin or Rosie?"

"Franklin doesn't exist anymore, it's just Rosie," I reminded her.

"Well, that's too bad. Franklin is welcome to come with us but we won't be taking Rosie."

"Excuse me?"

"I think it would be too confusing for Joey. Franklin is welcome..."

"Fuck you!" I rolled up my window and started the car.

"What's the matter?" Rosie asked. "Why can't I visit Joey?"

"It's not you, honey. Joey's grandma is a bitch!" I yelled loud enough for the wrinkled monster to hear. I pulled my car out of the parking spot and away from the store. We passed by the green van and witnessed Joey's small fists pounding against the glass. "Franklin! I want to play with Franklin!"

I was trying my damnedest to hold back my own tears. "Joey! Joey! I want to hang out with you!" Rosie screamed. My heart shattered.

About a week after Rosie's suspension was completed we attended her open house. I was anxious because Jade's mom would be there and I hoped that speaking to her might be the key to ending the bullying once and for all.

"I painted this one!" Rosie pointed out the masterpiece her teacher had mounted on the classroom wall. The look on her face was priceless. She grabbed my hand and dragged me to her desk, "Over there is my computer! Come on! You can read my journal entries!" She began scrolling through her Chromebook.

Rosie looked up and her expression changed. I turned my head to follow her gaze. Standing across from us was a tall girl with terrible posture, her skeletal frame hid by an over-sized black sweatshirt. The hood was pulled up, covering her hair, and the bottom hung loosely over a pair of boy's jeans.

"Is that Jade?" I asked.

Rosie nodded.

Next to Jade was a small woman around my age, sitting in a wheelchair. I walked up to her and introduced myself. "Hi, you must be Jade's mom. I'm Rosie's mom, Asterisk."

"Yes. Jade talks about Franklin all the time!"

"It's Rosie now, not Franklin. We have some serious issues with Jade's bullying this year." I told her about Rosie's suspension and what happened in the bathroom.

"I had no idea it was that bad. I'll talk to Jade about it," she promised. "Can I tell you a secret?"

"Um, sure?"

"Jade's had a little crush on Franklin since last year. Franklin wanting to be a girl has done a number on her. She misses him the way he was. I think Jade wants him to be her boyfriend."

I glanced back to Jade, and I realized she didn't look like a little girl; she looked like a boy. I bet she was struggling with gender issues of her own with lack of support. That's why she hated my child so much, it was envy. Noticing how meek her mother was, I had the gut feeling there was an abusive man at home ruling the roost.

"Let me give you my number," Jade's mom offered. "And if any new issues arise, send a text."

"I would appreciate that."

After exchanging numbers, we said goodbye to both Jade's mom and Rosie's teacher before heading back to the car. "What did Jade's mom say?" Rosie wanted to know.

"She won't let Jade bully you anymore."

Rosie let out a sigh of relief, "Good because I don't like her."

"Don't worry, honey," I said. "Jade's mom can't stand up for her daughter, anyway."

"Why not?"

"Because she's in a wheelchair!" I laughed.

Later that night I was scrolling through my social media when I saw Joey's mom, Tina, online. Having always been easygoing, I figured I could reach out to her about what had happened with her mother-in-law the weekend prior. I was hoping we could clear things up for the children's sake. I sent her a message.

"Hi Tina. Last weekend we had an unpleasant encounter with your mother-in-law when she arrived to pick up Rosie."

"Hello. Oh yeah, I heard. Sorry!"

"She refused to let Rosie play with Joey. She told me 'Franklin' was welcome but 'Rosie' wasn't. Franklin is Rosie now. I wanted to make sure this was a family decision and not just your mother-in-law's personal feelings."

"Franklin can come over anytime. Unfortunately, we can't have Rosie. Joey needs male friends and it would be too confusing for him."

My fingers slammed the keys. "Joey enjoys Rosie's companionship! I doubt he gives a shit if her shirts are pink instead of blue!"

"Franklin is welcome any time!"

"Fuck off!"

"Haha! Okay!"

Just like that, Rosie lost her best friend.

CHAPTER 3

Rosie and I became regulars at the LGBT Center. Not only did she continue her counseling sessions, we checked out several of their therapy groups and speakers. The first meeting we attended was a two-hour introduction for parents of young children going through transition. I left Rosie across the hall with other kids to play. Some of them were transgender, others siblings.

The first half was an introduction into "hormone therapy" and "hormone blockers." With a doctor's referral, blockers could allow Rosie the chance to put her puberty on hold for a few years. Meaning, she could transition into her teens without going through a physical change before making a permanent decision. With the new advancements in hormone treatments, Rosie didn't have to develop into the gender she had been assigned at birth. Instead, she might transition into the sex she related to. She didn't have to suffer from her gender dysphoria long term. With the help of estrogen, Rosie could develop breasts similar to those of cisgender girls. Estrogen would prevent unwanted hair growth on her body and face. Her hips would fill out with fatty tissues but her jaw line would remain soft. She'd develop similar characteristics to other girls in her age group. Once she turned eighteen, she would have the choice to medically alter her genitals to that of a female.

There was a short break, and the meeting continued. Parents of transitioning children made their way to the front of the room and told their stories. In that hour together, we laughed, cried and formed emotional bonds. When it ended, people scurried to their cars like cockroaches with the light turned on.

Each time we attended a meeting I exchanged phone numbers with parents of transgender kids Rosie befriended. Despite my best efforts I never made a play date happen outside the group.

Rosie grew bored with her therapy sessions and Ms. Jess relocated to another area. We chose not to continue on with a new counselor. The groups catered to new parents of transitioning kids and the information seemed to be on a loop. I learned more searching the internet on my own.

School ended for the summer and it relieved Rosie from Jade and all the bullying. I enrolled her in a new elementary in a different district and she planned to attend as female the following year, a fresh new start where nobody knew Franklin.

Summer started out slow for us, I worked a lot of hours and Rosie spent most of the time I was gone at home alone. I longed for a life partner and I know Rosie wished for a friend like her, someone she related to. So when Vivian showed up I thought she was everything we both needed and more.

CHAPTER 4

"**F**ive! Five! Hey Five!" her boisterous voice rang through the speaker of my car. "What-cha doin' girl?"

Oh my God, she cracked me up, and I loved the shit out of her. Vivian appeared out of thin air one night and never left. At the time it was all-encompassing, yet thrilling and magnetic. Even though I knew she was probably a sociopath, I didn't care.

"Ha haha! You kill me. I'm just leaving work. What are we doing tonight?" I asked.

"Ta-co Tues-day! Hurry home bitch. I'm putting on my makeup so I'll be hot for you when you get here. See you soon." Vivian hung up the phone, and I put the pedal to the metal.

Honestly, it happened so fast I can't really remember the exact details of how she came into my life, but I can recall the morning after. Now, I've woken up next to some beasts in my time but nothing prepared me for this. I rolled over in bed to find a full-grown man sleeping next to me wearing a pair of woman's panties. Again, not a first time on that front either, but this one had a little something special. If by special, I mean he was wearing a set of glittery pink acrylic nails. Upon further inspection, I discovered he also had a considerably large pair of breasts stuffed into a bra better looking than anything I had ever owned. He was Vivian.

Oh fuck!

I met Vivian online a few weeks prior and thought she could make a good mentor to Rosie, even though most of our conversations started out with the weird selfies she would send. Vivian was in her mid-thirties and in her second year of hormone therapy. We had been texting for a while and even though I explained I wasn't interested in dating her; I was still happy to be friends. I figured my friendship had plenty to offer, with me working in the beauty industry. I'd be happy to share some of my hacks.

The night before, I invited Vivian over for a few drinks and perhaps I had one too many.

"Hey, are you awake?" I asked my slumber buddy.

"Good morning girl," she greeted me in a nasal enhanced voice as high-pitched as one could muster while being burdened with an Adam's apple.

I looked under the covers to see myself naked. Glancing at the floor I spotted yesterday's clothes.

"Did we...?"

"Did we what?" Vivian asked me with the attitude of an eight-year-old girl.

"Do... anything? Sex? Did we have sex?" The question was more about "how" did we have it rather than "if." By the sharp throbbing sensation I was feeling in my vagina I had the sneaking suspicion I had been fingered by that exact set of acrylics.

"Please, girl! Don't be acting like you don't remember raping me last night!"

"Mommy?" I heard Rosie's voice.

Crap! I had some serious questions but they would have to wait for later. I grabbed my garb and quickly threw it on. Vivian reached for her T-shirt and did the same.

"Oh honey, I have a friend over, someone I want you to meet," I told Rosie as she appeared in the hallway to my bedroom. "This is Vivian. She is transgender too."

By the look on Rosie's face, you would have thought I brought home Santa Claus and the Easter Bunny at the same time. She had heard about full-grown transgender women before but she had never met one. Luckily she was so blown away by Vivian's presence she wasn't aware of the inappropriateness of the situation. Immediately, Rosie stuck to Vivian like a vulture to a dying elephant.

"Do you ladies want to grab an early lunch?" Vivian asked us, "My treat!"

"Sure," I agreed.

"Yes! Yes! Yes!" Rosie screamed.

"You drive, is that cool?" Vivian inquired. "My car is filled to the brim with clothing. It's been my home for the last six months."

"Yes, sure. Why are you living in your car?" I asked.

"Times have been hard since I came out. None of my friends or family can accept it. I was with my last girlfriend for five years. I told her in the beginning I wanted to be female but she didn't believe me. When I finally went forward with the change, she freaked out and threw me on the streets. I've been living in my car ever since."

"Oh wow, how terrible! I hate people! Rosie has been going through so much torment since she came out too. I completely understand what it is like," I empathized.

Once in my car we headed to the restaurant. While driving, Vivian grabbed my hand and started sensually rubbing it with her giant pink nails. Noticing the expression on Rosie's face, I gently pulled my hand away.

"I've been coming here with my family since I was a teenager. You guys will love this place! It's so good," Vivian promised.

Several miles later we pulled into an old industrial complex. The "restaurant" turned out to be a walk up counter with a few metal tables scattered outside. I watched Vivian climb out of my SUV and over a curb. She wore a pair of silver studded flats, a mid-length skirt, and an old T-shirt. The outfit didn't really go together, but I figured I'd save my "tips" for later. Immediately I observed strangers staring at her. I caught their gazes one by one and gave them each a look that said, "fuck off." This negative attention seemed new and I couldn't let my friend be gawked at.

Once at the counter, Vivian placed her order. This threw me for a loop because I had been accustomed to being in the company of men who always let the woman go first. I figured if we continued hanging out, I'd need to get used to it. After she finished ordering, I placed one for both Rosie and myself. When it came time to pay, Vivian gave the clerk her debit card.

"Thank you," I said to her with a smile. "Rosie, Vivian just bought you lunch, what do you say?"

But before Rosie could reply, Vivian's card was declined.

"That's okay!" I said, "Here!" I handed the clerk my credit card.

"Sorry, this is so embarrassing," Vivian said, pulling up banking information on her phone. "Shit! It looks like my car payment cleared today. I wasn't expecting that. What's the date? Is it the 10th already? I over drafted by $18. Crap, I left all my cash at your place. After lunch I'll swing back and grab a twenty to put in the bank."

"We can do it on the way home. I can loan you the money," I offered.

"You are amazing!" Vivian gushed. "You really are. I'm so glad I met you girls!"

CHAPTER 5

V ivian and I stayed up most of the second night talking and cuddling. Even though she wasn't the person I had been expecting to date, she was exciting. It thrilled me to have her in my life. She also had a softer side I related to.

"Before I came out, my body dysphoria haunted me. I would be out in public and notice a pretty girl and instantly hate her. I was jealous, I wanted to be her so bad. But now that I am 'her', I love myself," Vivian confessed.

I grabbed her hand and squeezed it. Then I looked at her face. She had the most piercing blue eyes I had ever seen. When she gazed at me it was as if she uncovered my soul. Vivian was unlike anyone I had met before. One minute she would use her "feminine" voice which reminded me of a gay man, and in the next, she would sound like a lumberjack. Her body language acted the same way. The first time I witnessed her crush an empty can of Pepsi with her bare hands, I felt in awe.

I didn't hear Vivian get up the following morning, I only made out the click of my front door behind her as she left. I remembered her saying she

31

had to work early the next day and wondered if she had even slept at all. Within seconds I was back to sleep.

My alarm rang a few hours later. I climbed out of bed and showered as Rosie ate her cereal. Forty-five minutes after that, we were almost out the door. As I searched for my keys, I noticed it.

Resting on a little side table was Vivian's purse. That bitch!

"Looks like Vivian will be back tonight," I told Rosie.

"I hope so! How do you know?"

"Look!" I said, pointing to the black velvet pouch. "She left her bag here."

I was on my lunch break later that day when my cell rang.

"Hey, girl," she greeted me, sounding somber.

"Hi, Vivian. How's your day going?"

"Dude, you won't believe it, this Mexican guy at my work tried to run me over with a bulldozer! Everyone saw it happen too!"

"Oh, my God, are you okay?"

"I'm fucking upset!" I could hear Vivian's voice crack as she cried, "I complained to my manager but he wouldn't do anything! I told him I would take it to Human Resources, so he sent me home for the day."

Her crying caught me off guard. She sounded like a cross between a yodeling hillbilly and a wounded cow. I wanted to be sympathetic, but it was just so strange, I had to hold back my laughter. "That isn't good, did he fire you?"

"No, he said I needed some time to cool off." Her somber tone suddenly changed to what I can only describe as her sexy voice. "Hey Five, I have a confession to make."

"Oh yeah? What's that?"

"I left my purse at your house, on purpose."

I laughed. "Yeah, I figured that! The oldest trick in the book."

"I wanted a reason to come back," she admitted. "I want to see you again."

"You didn't need an excuse. I'll be home around six. Come by, I'll make you dinner."

"Okay, I will go to the amusement park for a few hours and blow off some steam, I'll see you after."

Though Vivian was technically homeless, she still enjoyed several extravagances. She held season passes to almost every amusement park in Southern California and had upgraded them to include free meals. She had an active gym membership and tickets to sports arenas. Even her car was new. That bitch made being a hobo seem luxurious!

After work, I grabbed Rosie from daycare and hustled my way through the grocery store as fast as I could. I picked up some of my favorites: marinated chicken, corn on the cob and two bottles of wine. I knew it would take a while to get things prepped and on the barbecue and I didn't want to be late.

Once home, I opened some Cabernet, turned my stereo on and cooked. Rosie sat at the table playing a video game on her cell phone in anticipation. Every so often she would ask me if Vivian was here yet.

I went to refill my glass only to realize the bottle was empty. "Shit, I drank it that fast?" I asked, myself prior to opening the other. Glass in hand, I stepped onto the porch to check the grill. The chicken was fully cooked. I took the corn off moments later. I peeked at my cell phone, it was past 7:00 pm. Annoyed, I picked it up and shot Vivian a text. "Hey girl, dinner is ready, are you close?"

"I'm riding one last roller coaster then I'll be on my way."

I rolled my eyes and walked inside. "Are you hungry Rosie? Let me make you a plate."

"Yeah. Where is Vivian? I want to see my new friend!"

"She is running late. Eat your food and hop in the bath. She should be here when you get out," I said.

Close to 9:00 pm, Vivian finally appeared. Her long, strawberry blonde hair laid softly on her shoulders and she had on a fabulous shade of hot pink lipstick, but otherwise I didn't see much sign she was female. The T-shirt she wore was baggy and hid her breasts. On her legs was a faded pair of knee-length board shorts. She had on men's socks with her favorite sports team embroidered on them inside a torn set of Converse All-Stars.

While saying hello to Rosie and me, she sat at the kitchen table. I made her a plate of food and she ate a little of the chicken but claimed she was full from the lunch she had at the amusement park. She didn't apologize for being late, just rehashed the fork lift incident from earlier. I noticed she was still visibly shook up, so I let her continue.

After hearing the story three more times, I grew bored and looked at the clock to realize it was already past 10:00 pm and an hour after Rosie's bed time.

"Come on, Rosie," I said. "It's time to get into bed. Brush your teeth first."

"But mom! Vivian just got here. I want to hang out with her."

"Rosie, I let you stay up late. You already spent time together. Now say goodnight."

Hesitantly, my daughter followed my orders. Once she was in bed, I kissed her on the forehead and closed her door behind me as I exited the bedroom.

"Do you wanna smoke a joint?" Vivian asked.

"Sure." We headed outside and toked.

A little while later we made our way back into the apartment. "Hey Five, do you mind if I shower?"

"Not at all. You can even stay over again."

"Cool. I will run to my car and get some things."

Vivian returned with her belongings and tiptoed into the bathroom to start the water. I noticed she had left the door ajar. I was hoping she meant it as an invitation. I slid off my dress and peeked my head inside. "Mind if I join you?"

"Come on, girl."

After climbing into the shower, I let the hot water run down my body. I grabbed Vivian by the hips and pulled her towards me. As we locked lips, I anticipated the warmth from her tongue. She leaned into me and pressed her breasts onto my own before gently placing her hand on my crotch. She had a nice touch, despite the acrylics.

"Uhh!" she moaned. "Touch my clit!" This took me aback. As I tried to decipher what exactly she meant, she grabbed my hand and placed it onto her small erect penis.

I had read about hormone therapy and the impact it could have on a tranny's sex drive but experiencing it was new. I could tell the drugs caused some shrinkage, and the erection didn't seem as intense as that of a man. But still it functioned!

The warm water continued to run down both of our bodies as Vivian and I caressed each other. Soon we were close to completion, but I wasn't ready to end it just yet. Instead, I climbed out of the shower and grabbed my towel. I took another from the rack and handed it to my lady lover.

"I'll meet you in bed," I said with a wink. A moment later, Vivian joined me.

"Suck my titties!" she ordered. I did with a chuckle as she crawled on top of me and inserted herself. I took my hands off her breasts and grabbed her by the hips to guide her better inside of me. It posed a challenge because of her lack of firmness.

"Pinch my nipples!" she said.

I did my best to accommodate her. Eventually, she had us both in a position that seemed to keep our parts together. Vivian pumped herself into me short and fast. I looked up into one of the ugliest sex faces I had ever seen. Her eyes became slants and her jaw sat clenched in a crooked under-bite. She reminded me of Animal from The Muppet Show.

"You like that bitch? You like my clit fucking you?"

"Yeah, baby." I moaned.

"Tell me!"

"I love squeezing your giant tits, I want them all over me. Your clit feels so good, baby! Fuck me with your clit."

"You enjoy fucking a girl?" Vivian asked. "Can a woman fuck you better than anybody else can?"

"Yes, baby!" I lied.

Whatever would feed her ego was fine by me. This was probably the strangest sex I'd ever had, and it was just gross enough to get me off.

"I'm about to finish!" Vivian warned me.

"Me too, baby, come inside me!" I pleaded, but Vivian did not.

Instead, she pulled out her puny pecker and released her steamy "girl load" all over my tummy.

"You didn't have to pull out," I told her, when it was over. "My tubes are tied, I can't get pregnant."

"I can't knock you up, girl. Female hormones kill off sperm."

Oh crap!

"I didn't know that."

Suddenly I thought about Rosie and the hormone therapy she would be starting. Was I willing to continue to support her physically changing if it meant she wouldn't be able to have children? She was not emotionally mature enough to make that decision. I had been holding off on her legal name change for the same reason.

CHAPTER 6

The next morning, Vivian snuck off to work as she had the day prior. Rosie and I awoke to my alarm around 7:00 am. I made her a quick plate of scrambled eggs for breakfast before hopping in the shower. Once we were both dressed, we climbed into my car.

"Mommy, I heard you last night," Rosie said.

"You did? What did you hear?" I asked.

"You were loud. It scared me."

GULP.

"What did I say?"

"You said, 'Suck my titties.'"

Out of shock or sheer embarrassment, I let out a bellowing laugh that was highly inappropriate, and try as I might, I just couldn't stop more from coming. Tears slid down my cheeks. "Ha haha! That wasn't me. Haha! I didn't say that," I roared in between breaths. "Haha! That was Vivian!"

"Mommy! It's not funny! I opened your bedroom door, I looked inside and you weren't wearing clothes. Vivian was on top of you!"

My laughter ensued. Thoughts from the night before flooded through my brain. How disturbing it was on its own, and then to find out my poor child bore witness to the entire event.

"Stop laughing! I saw you both naked. You are gross! You are ugly when you are naked."

"Ha haha! I'm so sorry Rosie! Haha! I thought you were asleep! Haha! Why weren't you sleeping?"

"I couldn't, I was too excited because Vivian was here. But you know what? I don't like her anymore. I never want to see her again!"

"Oh honey, see? When I tell you it's your bedtime... Hahaha! If I tell you to go to sleep... Hahaha! You need to go to sleep, okay? I'm so sorry you had to witness that. But... When two grown-ups love each other, that's what they do. Haha! It's only natural."

Even though I felt disturbed that Rosie saw Vivian and I having sex, I thought maybe it wasn't such a horrible thing for her to understand that transgender women can find love too. Rosie was true to her word. She didn't view Vivian the same way after that. It took close to a week for her to even speak to Vivian again.

Sometime later in the week, I received a frantic call from my lady.

"Can I come by tonight?" she asked, her voice trembling.

"Sure, what's up? Everything okay?"

"I quit my job!" she confessed.

A cloud of dread encircled me. Vivian was already living out of her car and financially suffering, She couldn't afford to not be working. Job placement could be a difficult task for transgender persons. "What happened?"

"Well, remember that asshole Mexican guy that tried to run me over?"

"Yeah..."

"He rushed into Human Resources and told them I was prejudice! Me! I'm transgender!"

"Oh, my God, that is the most preposterous thing I have ever heard," I said.

"I told them they were being prejudiced against me! They didn't care! They took his side!" she yelled through her tears.

"I'm so sorry Vivian. What will you do without a paycheck?"

"They are letting me cash out my vacation pay and then I'm starting my seasonal job at the carnival."

"The carnival? You are a 'carny'?" I asked with a chuckle.

"Yup! All summer long," she said.

"Well, I wouldn't be upset about the construction job, you have time to search for something new. Don't worry, you will find a better position with an employer who deserves you."

"Aww, I love you, girl!"

"I love you too," I said.

Vivian arrived at my apartment not long after our phone call. It had been days since Rosie had said more than two words to her, but Vivian had a plan.

"Hi Rosie!" she said, "I brought you something."

Rosie looked up from her video game and caught sight of Vivian holding a pack of Pokemon cards. Rosie was collecting and obsessing over those dumb things. That bitch had found her sweet spot.

"Wow! Let me have them!" Rosie said.

"What do you say?" I asked.

"Thank you!"

And just like that Vivian had bought back my daughter's love.

CHAPTER 7

That following weekend Vivian worked her summer job with the traveling carnival. The first location was in a city two hours away. Vivian wouldn't be coming back at night. We had become so close in such a short time that our first week apart was torture. Still, Vivian called me every morning before work and every night before she fell asleep to recap her day.

"Hey Five!"

"Hey girl, hey!" I greeted my new love.

"I had the worst customer today! She was a gross fat beast with terrible eyebrows!"

"Aww, I'm sorry, baby. Was that old bag rude to you?"

"She kept calling me sir! I looked cute today too with my makeup on. She ate more than half her meal, then she tried to return it by saying it wasn't fresh. Please, If you don't want something, you bring it back before you scarf it down!"

"No kidding!" I agreed.

"Anyway, I corrected her three times! I even pointed out my name badge that had 'Vivian' printed on it!"

"Ugh. I hate people!"

"She asked for my manager. When he came over, the ugly bitch kept talking about me, right in front of my face. She was saying things like; 'he' wouldn't give me my money back and 'he' is rude."

"She's fucking ignorant."

"I know, right? Anyway, Five, how was your day?"

"It sucked until now. I love talking to you," I said.

"Aww! I love talking to you too, Five!"

"Can you come back to town now? I wanna cuddle you."

"I so wish. I will catch you next week when I get back. I want to take you on a date." Vivian said.

"Oh, you do?" I asked. "Where would we go?"

"You plan the sitter and I'll plan the date."

"Okay. A week from Monday."

"I want to get dressed up for you." she said.

Even though I found Vivian most attractive when she looked like a man; I realized being female was who she felt inside and what made her happy so I played along. "I love seeing you all dressed up, babe."

"I do my makeup better than most girls. Bitches don't know how to do their makeup right. I get complimented all the time when I'm done up," she boasted.

Chuckling, I replied, "I bet you do."

"I want to climb on top of you, make out, and get each other's makeup all over our bodies. That would be so hot!"

"I always want you on top of me!"

"I'll be dreaming of that tonight, girl. Sweet dreams."

"Be safe!" I lectured.

"After we hang up, I'll send you a map of my location."

Although I didn't like her being gone, I slept a little sounder knowing where she parked for the night.

CHAPTER 8

One perk of dating a transgender girl is sharing clothes and makeup. One downside is getting your underwear mixed up in the wash.

I have to say what I miss the most about Vivian were our days home alone together. After sending Rosie to school that Monday, the two of us put on our faces together. Vivian sat at my dining room table with the double-sided vanity mirror I gifted her, while I stood in the adjoining bathroom using the built-in mirror.

"Do you like this lipstick?" she called out, and I happily inserted my opinion. I always preferred the lighter shades on her. Not only because they suited her skin tone the best, but because I wasn't a fan of her dark kiss marks smudged all over me.

"I hate my facial hair!" she regularly complained. "It grows back too fast and makes me look like a man. I can shave it, and an hour later it's back. Sometimes I just want to peel my face off! I hate it that much!"

"I wish you could get laser hair removal."

"Me too, but I can't afford it right now. It could change my life."

"Here, let me do your makeup," I offered.

"You think you can hide it?" she asked.

"Perhaps," makeup artistry was part of my profession. I worked on Vivian for about 30 minutes but wasn't happy with the results. That afternoon I secretly researched the best concealer to hide facial hair on transgender women and ordered it from Amazon. I gave it to her later in the week.

"Ooh, I love it!"

"Also," I said, handing Vivian my spare house key, "I want you to have this."

"Are you asking me to move in?"

"I don't like you staying in your car. It scares me, you being out there alone at night."

"I can take care of myself. I'm smart!"

"I know, it would just sit better with me if you had an option," I said.

I emptied one of my spare closets and let Vivian move in her belongings. When she put her favorite pillow on my bed, I must admit it was comforting.

Our sex life was in full swing and we made each other orgasm every day. Though she didn't have much left "downstairs," Vivian was a professional with her hands and soon I had convinced her to remove her nasty acrylics for gel polish, which I agreed to change out for her every few weeks.

After fooling around that afternoon, we were holding hands naked on top of my bed. One of my cats jumped up near our heads looking for affection. Faster than the free fall from a snapped bungee cord, Vivian's arm swung out and launched my pet onto the floor.

"What the hell, Vivian?" I screamed.

"What?"

"You can't treat my cat that way!"

"Oh, I'm sorry. She startled me. I was half asleep and I'm allergic to cats."

"You're allergic to cats?" I asked, confused by this confession. Vivian had spent most of her time at my place for over a month and she had not complained until now. She hadn't sneezed either.

"Yeah. I don't know what it is about your cats, they must be extra clean or something because they rarely bother me, but other cats always have."

"Just try to be less aggressive next time."

Vivian agreed.

We snoozed for an hour longer and then Vivian got up to smoke a bowl of marijuana. I cracked open a beer and sat across from her at the dining room table.

"Rosie will be home soon, we should go get something to eat," I said.

"I know a great place she will love."

Vivian threw on her "token" T-shirt, medium length skirt and studded flats ensemble. I decided on a cool summer dress and kimono.

We swung by the school and picked up my daughter. Vivian drove in her now empty car. She had an obsession for punk rock music and blasted it as loud as her factory stereo would play. All the while she gripped my hand into her own, every so often looking deep into my eyes and giving me the "gushy" emotion of being in love.

When we reached the front of the restaurant, I noticed it was a popular eatery because the lot was filled with cars. Vivian drove around the building a few times to find a place to park. Once settled, she hopped out and jetted to the entrance without ever looking back. Rosie and I followed her inside. It would be a challenge dating a girl in more ways than one. Especially since I had become so accustomed to having my car door opened for me by a gentleman. It was a luxury I'd have to learn to forgo.

Inside the restaurant, we made our way to the back of a huge line.

"I will take a medium veggie pizza, Rosie what do you want?" Vivian asked.

"I want chicken wings!"

"Cool," Vivian said, handing me a $20 bill. "We will meet you upstairs."

I watched in shock as the two of them made their way up to a second story to find a place to sit while leaving me alone in the giant line. Realizing what happened set me off, and I felt my blood pressure rising.

"Oh well," I thought to myself, at least there was beer.

After several minutes passed, I made it to the front of the line. "One medium veggie pizza, an order of wings, a roasted veggie salad and a pitcher of beer," I ordered.

"Oh, I'm sorry, you can't get the beer here. Get it from the bar," the cashier informed me, pointing to a line on the opposite side of the hall that was even longer than this one.

Great, just fucking great.

"That comes to $31.68."

I glanced down at the twenty-dollar bill. That bitch hadn't given me enough money for all of our food. I handed the woman my credit card, and she gave me back a receipt containing our order number.

I walked over to the bar. Why would Vivian ditch me like this? Maybe she felt embarrassed to stand in line in her skirt? That must be it. Why else did she need to sit down? I was trying to give her the benefit of the doubt.

At least fifteen minutes had passed before I made it to the front of the line. Once the beer was poured, I grabbed the pitcher, two frosty mugs, and headed upstairs. I needed a drink before I bit Vivian's head off.

"Hey girl!" she said, as I brought the drinks. "Here, go get the food!" she ordered Rosie, handing her the receipt.

"Rosie kept asking if she could get it," Vivian said, noting the scornful look on my face.

"Be careful, don't drop it!" I said, as Rosie bound towards the stairs. Once she was out of earshot, I turned my attention back to Vivian.

"What the hell? That's fucked up of you to leave me in line! You should have been the one doing the ordering."

"Why? I was watching your kid for you."

"I can take care of my own kid. That was so rude," I scolded her.

"What? I gave you money. Don't treat me like a man."

Flustered, I poured myself a beer and washed a blood pressure pill down with it. A few minutes and several sips later I was calmer. Rosie arrived with the food.

"Here, try this!" Vivian ordered, putting a small piece of pizza on my plate. I couldn't deny that it was delicious.

"See, I told you you would love this place!"

I was in a better mood after food and drink so when Vivian suggested that we make our way a few blocks to the water; I obliged. You know, as long as we could stop at the liquor store. To make it up, Vivian entered the store alone and came out carrying two large bottles of Corona.

With our beers hidden inside paper bags, we sipped as we walked down a long stairway leading to the coast. The sun was setting as we crossed over a set of train tracks. Vivian and I sat on a large rock overlooking the water while Rosie made her way further to the edge of the beach. She took off her shoes and waded in the frigid salt water.

The sky was a spectacle of warm colors. I could sense a chill in the air and Vivian instinctively grabbed my body close to hers and wrapped half of her hooded sweatshirt around me. She looked deeply into my eyes and kissed me. I knew that night would stick with me a long time.

Just as the sun had disappeared under the line of the water, Vivian called

Rosie to join us. "I bet your mom might have some change," she said.

"Actually, I do." I reached into my bag, handing Vivian several pennies and a nickel.

"Come on!" she said to Rosie, "I hear the train coming!"

The three of us made our way to the tracks and watched as Vivian laid out the coins on a rail one by one. "Okay! Step away," she instructed. "Rosie, get further back!"

Just as Rosie jumped a safe distance backward, we heard the loud sirens and rumbling of the train. A gust of wind slapped our bodies as the machine hurled its way past us. It felt powerful yet frightening all at once. We could hear the scraping from the metal as the crushing wheels hit the coins. They flew with incredible force into a patch of rocks nearby.

When the train had gone, Vivian scrambled back to collect the smashed pieces of copper and silver. She handed one coin to each of us. The crushed metal was warm to the touch. I tucked mine into the small side pocket of my purse for safekeeping as we made our way back to the car.

CHAPTER 9

I cleaned up my workstation and headed to the parking garage. Vivian arrived home from her carnival job late the night before, after I was already fast asleep. It had been over a week since we had spent any time together and I was missing her like a cure for scabies. It was Monday evening and Vivian and I were going on our official first date. I had one hour to get to the apartment and change before the babysitter was to arrive. I climbed into my SUV and hauled ass home.

I flew down the freeway as fast as I could. Once through my front door, I wrapped my arms around my girlfriend and planted a giant kiss on her crooked face. I took a deep breath from her neck and inhaled the scent of her floral shampoo. Damn had I missed her.

"I'm so happy to see you! You look so beautiful!" I told my bitch.

"Thanks baby girl! I missed you too!" Vivian had on a mid-length sequined gun metal dress and a faux fur shawl draped across her shoulders. On her feet was the biggest pair of black patent leather stilettos I had ever seen, by both size and height! They reminded me of something Ronald

McDonald might wear if he went drag. On the toe of the right pump I noticed a long scratch. Vivian caught me eyeing it, "My ex girlfriend was less than thrilled when I brought these shoes home," she said. "She wasn't supportive of my transformation so she chucked them at the wall. They left a huge smudge on the paint too."

"Good," I said, "Serves her right."

"Go get ready or we will be late!"

After giving her one more kiss on the cheek, I ran to my closet and put on my favorite little black dress. I was excited to see it fit me looser these days. The front was low cut, revealing my ample bosom. It had a tie around the waist that hugged my curves in all the right places. I threw on a high pair of lime green platforms and finished the look off with muted pink lips and a smokey eye. I let my long blond curls cascade down my back. Yup, I was a babe.

"Oh Asterisk, I love you in those heels!" Vivian complimented me. "When you are tall, it makes me seem more 'believable'." I wasn't sure if it was a compliment. Before I could decide, the doorbell rang. It was the babysitter. I kissed Rosie goodbye, told her to be a good girl, and we were out the door.

Once in the car, Vivian lit a joint and bumped her stereo at full volume. She passed the pot my way and grabbed my left hand, holding it snugly. She turned and smiled, before bringing my fingers to her lips for a smooch. "I love you, girl."

We pulled up to what Vivian said was her all-time favorite Italian restaurant. Before we entered, she gave me a deep kiss with tongue action. "I haven't been here in years, I wonder if anyone will recognize me." It didn't take long before someone had.

"Hi, John," a woman's voice greeted her. "It's been a while. How are you?"

They continued with their pleasantries for a few moments before the woman took our order. Once she left Vivian leaned into my ear, "She's never seen me as 'her'."

"She didn't act too surprised."

"I slept with her once," she admitted.

"She's cute, but I'm hotter."

The food arrived, and it was just as fabulous as my girlfriend promised. Or perhaps the munchies from the marijuana made me believe it was. I finished my entire plate like a little piggy.

Once Vivian paid the bill, we set out to our next destination; a quick stop at the closest liquor store for a six-pack of beer and then up a hillside to her favorite lookout point.

High-heeled, we hiked down a dark and deserted dirt path to a huge slab of cement on top of a hill surrounded by trees. Below us was a canyon that stretched on forever. In the distance was the black outline of a large mountain.

"I used to come up here with my buddies to drink. We called this 'the stage'."

Vivian used the back of her lighter to open herself a beer. After taking a sip, she nodded her head in approval and set it on a slab of concrete. She picked up a second bottle of brew and popped the top for me. As I sipped my own, Vivian put hers to her burgundy painted lips and chugged it. That was surprising because in all the time we'd spent together, I'd never seen her drink more than a few beers at any occasion let alone pound one like a dying hooker.

My date released an enormous belch which echoed across the canyon, and then she threw her beer bottle right down into it. It took the container longer to fall to the bottom of the mountain and shatter than it did for Vivian to consume it!

"Holy shit! Nobody would ever know you didn't go to college," I said in astonishment, reacting to her childish antics.

Vivian laughed.

I wasn't certain if it had to do with her seeing an old flame that night or what, but Vivian's femininity had all but vanished. In that moment I was staring into the face of one rude ass "dude." She popped the top off of another beer and offered me a second, but I had to decline as I was only a sip into my original. Speaking more like a California surfer than a gay man, Vivian continued to open up about her past.

"A few weeks after I left my ex girlfriend, I was feeling bad about myself so I dressed like a guy and headed to a bar. I wanted to see if I 'still had it.' So I hit on the hottest chick there. She was into me and took me back to her place to hook up. I pulled my shirt off, and she noticed my breasts."

"Oh, my God, shut up!" I exclaimed.

"She asked me why I had tits. I told her 'I used to be fat.'"

"Ha haha!" I spit my beer out; I was laughing so hard some of it even came fizzing out of my nose, "You told her you used to be fat?"

"Yeah."

"THAT IS THE MOST AWESOME THING I HAVE EVER HEARD!"

"She didn't think so. She found me on social media a few days later as 'her' and flipped out. I guess it messed with her head. She told me I was an 'asshole' and that she never wanted to see me again. But I didn't care, I just needed the self-esteem boost, you know?"

Vivian guzzled her second beer just as fast as she had the first. I decided I should try to keep up with her, so we consumed the rest of the six-pack in about twenty minutes.

"Check it out!" I pointed to the mountain across from us. It was on fire. You could see the outline from the smoke stretching for miles. We sat cuddling together on the concrete slab and watched the distant flames for what seemed like hours. It was frightening yet spectacular to view. It was the same way I felt about Vivian. She was a real freak but damn, I was falling in love with her, anyway.

I had spent so many years staying home and taking care of Rosie on my own that I had almost forgotten what fun was. And with Vivian, fun was being bad! But not that bad... I looked down at my phone; it was almost midnight. "We better get back home Vivian, the babysitter needs to leave soon."

I put the five remaining bottles into the six-pack holder to take back with us.

"Here, let me see those." Vivian took them out of my hand.

Wow! Was she really doing something polite and carrying them to the trash for me? Nope. Instead, Vivian grabbed a bottle out of the carrier and launched it as far as she could over the cliff.

"What are you doing?" I asked, "You are disrupting the environment. Animals live there. Stop!"

Vivian was in a trance, she didn't acknowledge me at all. Actually, she didn't stop until every bottle and the holder were long down the mountain.

Once in the car, Vivian leaned into me and put her purple lips onto mine. Her face was soft and her tongue tasted of beer, which I loved. Regretfully, I had to stop her when I remembered the time.

We made it back to my place at midnight on the dot. I hurried inside while Vivian parked. After excusing the sitter for the evening, I ran into the bathroom to empty my booze-filled bladder. While washing my hands, I glanced into the mirror and shrieked. Vivian had smeared her dark lipstick across my face. Great! How long had it been there? Did it happen when we kissed before dinner or after we left the canyon?

As Vivian entered my apartment, I intended to lecture her about informing me the next time she decided to graffiti my face but stopped short when she touched me. She untied my dress, pulled it open and directed me to the bed. I helped her tug her own clothing off as we made out. Being aware of what turned her on; I fondled her firm breasts, making my way to her nipples. I used my nails to tickle them until her 'clit' was hard. Vivian put her face on mine and kissed me. When she inserted one of her magic fingers into my pussy, I could sense myself moistening.

"You are so wet," she whispered.

I giggled, "You make me this way."

Sweat and lipstick were everywhere. Soon we were both decorated like Easter eggs. As had become our ritual, she rolled on top of me and I helped her insert herself inside. Only this time something was different.

"You like my hard cock?" she asked.

I was a little disconcerted by her choice of wording, but once again, I played along.

"Oh yeah baby, I love your cock inside of me. I love the way you feel! You are so hard!"

Possibly, it was from seeing the old familiar face of her previous lover. Perhaps she was just heavily intoxicated and forgot at the moment she was transgender. Maybe she was fantasizing that I was the hot chick she fucked after her ex. I'll never know. But I came an ocean that night!

CHAPTER 10

The next morning I was hung over, which was a bummer because I had a hectic time at work. I called Vivian on my lunch break.

"Hey baby!" she addressed me.

"Hi girl, I feel like shit today, can it just be over already? I just need to come home and be with you."

"Aww. I'm at the park riding roller coasters right now. What time will you be off?" she asked.

"I should be home around 6:00 pm."

"Let's meet at the apartment, we can grab dinner later. I love you Five! Mwah!"

My long work day finally came to a close. I stopped at the daycare and picked up Rosie on my way home. My gut had been aching all day. I needed a healthy salad to coat it and a small glass of something alcoholic to fix my head. Once at the apartment I opened the door to find Vivian asleep on the couch. Her clothes and shoes were strewn around the floor and my kitchen table was turning into her personal vanity. Cosmetics, purses, random receipts, books and her giant water pipe consumed it. I let out a heavy groan as I moved the bong discreetly into her closet.

"Hey girl," she mumbled.

"Hi beautiful. I am famished, can we go eat now?" I begged, disappointed.

I had been expecting she would be ready to leave when we arrived.

Vivian sat up and I realized she merely had on a minuscule pair of lace panties without a top or bra. Rosie noticed at the same moment and gawked at Vivian's bulging breasts. I threw a T-shirt her way, and she slipped it over her chest.

"I need to pee before we leave," I headed to the restroom.

When I returned Vivian was taking a gigantic bong toke. "We are going to Clucks for dinner! Have you ever been there?"

"Uh, no. What is Clucks?" I asked, uncertain of Vivian's culinary choice.

She released a colossal cloud of cannabis smoke and proceeded, "Oh, my God, girl! It's the greatest fried chicken ever!"

"Oh, no. No, I'd prefer not. My stomach has been troubling me all day and..."

"Rosie really wants to go to Clucks, don't you?" She looked to my daughter for assistance.

"Yes! Please Mommy, can we eat at Clucks?"

"My treat!" Vivian offered. "I want to buy Rosie Clucks for the first time!"

I gave in. "Fine," I said, figuring there would have to be something I could eat. Boy was I mistaken. Clucks turned out to be a fast-food joint. There weren't any salads or fermented beverages anywhere. Great.

"Can I order a 'grown up' meal?" Rosie asked.

"No Rosie, kid's meals are only $2.50!" Vivian said. "I'm buying yours too, Five! What will you have?"

"Oh, nothing for me, thank you."

"What? Why not? Clucks is yummy! You gotta try it!" Vivian demanded.

"I'm sure it is, but my stomach is just to upset. The last thing I need right now is grease."

I found an unoccupied table and parked my rear. Vivian ordered for herself and Rosie.

"You sure you don't want some of my fries?" she asked.

"No thanks." I sat at the table and zoned out while the two of them dined.

"I kinda feel like a bitch for dragging you here," Vivian confessed.

"Don't, it's cool," I lied. Although I was dissatisfied by how the evening was turning out, I figured I would try to make the best of it. Vivian was leaving town to work the carnival again in the morning and I wouldn't see her for another week. I just craved to spend time with her. Plus, I could toast an avocado sandwich later. "Do you mind if we stop for some rose' on the way home?"

"You drink a lot, girl! But yeah, I suppose I can stop if you want to."

Vivian and I spent the evening cuddled up on my sofa watching TV as I savored my wine. When I was sure Rosie was fully asleep in her room, I reached over to fondle Vivian's breasts. She followed suit. After a long make-out session, we both came and fell asleep in each other's arms.

The week without my love seemed to drag on endlessly. Life wasn't the same without her. When she was around, she kept me entertained and laughing with her witty sense of humor. She could recount stories all night long. My black and white world seemed alive with color when she was in it. As she had done the week before, she called me every morning to say hello and in the evening before she went to sleep in her car. I stood by until midnight or later just to receive her calls. The days crawled on slowly.

"Hey Five!" she greeted me after one of her late nights. "Guess what? I scored us baseball tickets! We can take Rosie! Her favorite team is playing."

"Awesome! Sounds like a blast. I've never been to a sports game before," I blurted out. "Rosie loves them; she has only gone with her dad."

"The venue was having a special sale, guess how much I paid for 3 tickets? Guess!"

"I don't know."

"SEVEN DOLLARS!"

"Wow, that's amazing!"

"Not each, total! And Rosie gets a free jersey of her favorite player!"

"Perfect score, Vivian!"

"And you know what else? We will order nachos, they have the best nachos!"

"I fucking love you!"

CHAPTER 11

It was close to 1:00 am when Vivian made it home from the carnival that week. She called me thirty minutes before arriving. "I'm starving, girl! I'm gonna stop off and grab some food."

"Are you sure? I can make you something. How about queso? You have those frozen taquitos I can heat." I had been staying up indulging in my favorite pastime, alcoholism, while waiting for my lady love to get home. I was wide awake, excited and ready for a good time. Cooking was an excellent way to pass the rest of the hour. I enjoyed helping Vivian. I lived to make her happy.

"You are so awesome, babe! See you soon."

Blushing, I twisted the knob to the gas burner and prepped the food. Once everything was heating on low, I headed out to the porch with my glass of wine and lit up a cigarette. I wasn't a regular smoker but every once in a while, when under the influence, I enjoyed a couple. The gate to my porch swung open. Putting on the food took more time than I had noticed. I was busted!

"Gross! Why are you smoking again? I hate those things, Asterisk!" Vivian lectured me. "I thought you said you would stop."

"I am," I lied, "right after this one. Hey, food is almost ready!"

Vivian skipped the kiss "hello," and marched into the house for dinner. After a few puffs, I put out my cancer stick and joined her inside. I washed my hands and sat down next to my lady love and her enormous plate of Mexican food. She reached out and took my hands looking me deep in the eyes, "I love you, girl. I wish you would quit smoking. It will kill you and I want you to be around a long time, okay? If we are going to be together, you can't die off before me."

"I'm trying!"

Vivian rehashed her day. I was too drunk to pay attention and more interested in having her join me for some wine. She declined and gobbled her food.

"I'm going to sleep." She plopped on my bed and closed her eyes. I rolled on top of her and kissed her neck.

"Ew! You stink like cigarettes, Asterisk! Leave me alone, I'm tired."

"Oh, come on, I wanna play," I begged.

"Gross! Stop it! You are acting like a man!" she said. I calmed her by running my nails across her back. She snored. Feeling defeated, I gave up and joined her.

Something jolted me out of my dreams. "What the hell is that?" Vivian shrieked.

"Mommy, what's that noise?" Rosie asked from across the hall.

I was still drunk and a bit groggy. "Huh? I don't know!"

"The house is on fire!" Vivian jumped out from under the covers. "It's the smoke alarm! Get up! Come on!"

"Ahhhhh!" Rosie screamed. I was out of it, but there didn't seem to be a reason for such distress. Yes, it was in fact the smoke alarm but there weren't flames. "Calm down you two," I said, while climbing out of bed. I pulled a chair up to the alarm and removed the battery. I inspected the apartment for signs of a fire and encouraged the girls to go back to sleep. A few hours later the alarm sounded again. This time the sun was up.

"I smell something coming from the kitchen. Do you think the neighbors burned their breakfast?" I asked Vivian. "It smells like it's coming from inside the walls. Maybe it's electrical?"

"You need to call maintenance."

"Wait a second," I said, while taking another glance through the kitchen. "Holy shit!"

"What is it?" Vivian asked.

"The gas burner is on low! It's been on all night! This pan has been sitting on it. I bet it's destroyed, the bottom is black!"

"Damn it, Asterisk! You left the burner on? Oh, my God! You could've killed us!" Vivian shouted in her 'man' voice.

"Shit!" I said, realizing the danger. "You are at fault too Vivian. I was drunk! I'm your responsibility when I'm intoxicated! This has never happened before."

"Whatever, you need to be in control of your own damn self!" Vivian made her way into the bathroom and sat on the toilet, leaving the door cracked. I noticed Rosie peek her head out of her bedroom and across the hall. She was looking in on Vivian and had her eyes glued on to her crotch.

"Ew, Rosie! Stop that!" I yelled. "Vivian, shut the door! Rosie is being creepy!"

The water ran and Vivian's shower dragged on for over an hour. She must have been making up for lost time from living in her car. Suddenly, strange sounds emerged from inside.

HAWK! Splack! HAWK! Splack!

I knocked on the door. "Are you okay in there?"

"I'm fine!"

HAWK! Splack!

Vivian was hawking loogies in my shower! When I realized, my stomach bubbled, and I did my best to hold in the contents. The noise intensified as did my queasiness. She must have taken a theater class in high school because she reached into her gut for full intensity, just as an acting coach would instruct his student.

HAWK! Splack!

She could have been a gold medalist in the Mucus Olympics! Vivian didn't need a tissue, she had my drain. When she finished, I entered to find little gray specs of phlegm splatted onto my shower walls resembling splashes of paint. I cleaned them up; I didn't want Rosie bathing in it.

"I'm off to work," I said to Vivian. "Rosie doesn't have school today. I told her she could stay home alone instead of going to daycare if she wanted."

"No school, huh?" Vivian asked. "I'm going to Happy Hills amusement park today. I've got an extra pass, she can come with me if she wants. Rosie do you enjoy roller coasters?"

"No! I hate them!"

"You hate them? Why? Are you scared?"

"Yes!" Rosie admitted. "I only like little kid rides."

"Oh, come on Rosie, you can ride with me. It will be fun! Don't be a baby!"

"Okay."

I left for work as the two of them headed to the amusement park. Vivian sent me photos throughout the day. I returned home from work that night to find it empty.

"Where are you guys?" I asked through text.

"Just one more ride and we will head home."

"Vivian, you are an hour away and it's Rosie's bedtime!"

"Just one more ride. Relax, Five."

It was after 11:00 pm when they walked through my front door. I sent Rosie to bed without a bath and scolded Vivian. She pressed her finger to my lips to hush me. I felt the moistness of her tongue on my neck and then she placed my hand onto her throbbing crotch. I forgot what I was saying.

One orgasm later, I decided I could forgive her.

CHAPTER 12

It was Taco Tuesday again, my favorite time of the week! Vivian still had a few nights left before returning to the carnival. She spent an hour online job searching that morning and then the rest of her day smoking pot, sleeping on my couch and making messes. Once again I arrived home from a long day of work to discover what appeared to be the destruction left by a tornado inside my apartment.

"Seriously?" I asked my six foot tall 'fun house'. "Listen, I know you can't afford to help with rent but I would appreciate it if you could at least tidy up once in a while."

"Hey Rosie!" Vivian said, "Take the trash out for your mom!"

"What? Why do I have to?" Rosie asked.

"Well, it is your chore," I reminded her.

"When you finish, empty the dishwasher," Vivian ordered.

Really? This was her way of helping? By telling my child to do chores? I let out a sigh and cleaned up my dining room table. Once it was clear of Vivian's belongings, I sprayed it with wood polish before proceeding into the kitchen and wiping crumbs off the counter tops.

"Chill out," Vivian said. "Let's try to have a good time tonight. It's Taco Tuesday!"

That bitch had a point, plus I could use some margaritas. "Fine! Let's go!"

She drove, so I'd be able to guzzle my fill of tequila at the restaurant, and on the way she blasted her favorite music. It was a mix of old punk rock and ska, the same stuff she listened to in high school. I think that was part of her appeal. She reminded me of the stoner kids I used to hang out with in 10th grade. Ever since giving birth to Rosie, I had been a boring old mom, but when I was around Vivian, I was free to be an immature asshole.

Though we arrived early, there was still a line at the Mexican place. The three of us sat on the bench outside the joint to wait. Passersby gawked at Vivian but she didn't seem to notice. I caught restaurant patrons whispering to each other after eyeing her. I glared at anyone I could make eye contact with, anyone who disrespected my girl.

It seemed like it progressed further than that. They weren't just disrespecting Vivian; they were disrespecting Rosie too, and anyone else who wasn't cisgender. I'm not sure why, but I decided it was my obligation to stand up for transgender people everywhere!

A little while afterward, we were seated inside. The three of us pigged out on as many chicken tacos as we could stuff into our fat faces. I guzzled a good three or four margaritas. Vivian had only one. After dinner, we headed back down to what was now "our spot" by the train tracks overlooking the ocean. On the way, we made a quick stop at the local liquor store. This time I ran in and snagged two big beers and a box of juice for Rosie. Being buzzed, I concluded I could go for a smoke and bought a pack of cigarettes too. I tucked the cancer sticks inside my handbag and flung the rest of our treats into Vivian's car.

At the beach, we grabbed our goodies and descended a never ending staircase. From a distance, the sunset was larger than life. Five minutes later, we reached the bottom and cut across the tracks as the sun went down. The timing was impeccable. It felt like we were on another planet. As she had before, Rosie took off her shoes and raced into the water. Vivian used the back of a lighter to open our beers. We each took a sip. I reached into my purse, pulled out a cigarette and grabbed the lighter still lingering in Vivian's hand. I almost had it lit when there was a loud shatter.

"What the hell?" I asked. I looked down to see Vivian's empty hand. She had thrust her forty ounce bottle of beer onto the rocks. "This is fucking bullshit! You obviously like those things better than me!" I watched as she jumped up and took off sprinting into the dusk. Stunned, I took a drag off my smoke. Rosie was still playing in the waves and hadn't heard a sound. The sun was now setting and there was a dark shadow cast all around us. I glanced back to Vivian to see she had crossed the tracks and was now making her way up the stairs.

Her sudden rage unnerved me and I chose not to follow. Instead, I would allow her some space to cool down. I hadn't witnessed behavior like this from her before. Her overreaction triggered something in me and I wept. This was a red flag, and Vivian had to go. If I didn't end things now, I knew they would escalate. Next time that bottle could be aimed at me... or worse.

I waited until the sun had disappeared and it turned cold. I called Rosie out of the water. "Where is Vivian?" she asked.

"I'm not sure. Put on your shoes."

I picked up my phone and sent Vivian a text. "You are scaring me. It is not okay for you to abandon us at the beach like this. Please, at least order us an Uber."

Vivian responded, "I'm still here. Meet me at the car and I'll drive you home." I was wary of riding with Vivian after her obvious display of aggression and I didn't want to let Rosie in on what happened. I hoped Vivian would have recovered, and it seemed she had.

We traveled the eighteen miles back to my apartment in silence. Vivian didn't know it yet, but she wouldn't be staying. We approached my parking garage, and I asked her to back her car in. She accompanied me inside.

Once through my door, I handed her a plastic bag. "Here, I'll help you pack." I looked over to Rosie, "Go take a long bath."

Vivian didn't say a word, and she didn't make eye contact until after she loaded her car. Returning my key, she leaned in for a hug. I interjected. "Nope! No thanks! Please go." She raised her arms up in defeat and left my apartment.

A short time later my cell phone rang. I ignored it and put Rosie to bed. Afterwards I noticed several text messages, I deleted them without reading. It saddened me how it ended; I knew deep down I had done the right thing. I had withdrawn from an abusive relationship before it became violent; I was making progress in life. Good for me!

Just as I was about to fall asleep there was a knock on my door. It was her. Damn it!

"Asterisk! I know you are there, please let me in! I'm sorry!"

I ignored her, but the pounding continued. "Please, baby girl, I wasn't trying to scare you. You mean more to me than anything, can we talk?" She stood at my door sobbing and tapping for what seemed like ages. Worried she would wake Rosie, I gave in and let her back inside. Her tears were like waterfalls as she shook. I walked her into my room, put her on my bed and soothed her until she fell asleep. The next morning I helped her carry her stuff back in.

CHAPTER 13

"Y̲ou know I'm crazy, right?" Vivian asked, after inhaling a gargantuan bong toke.

"Stop it! You are not crazy. You are incredible," I assured her. "If other people can't understand you, that's their issue. I think you are perfect the way you are. You are my favorite person ever!"

"No Asterisk, I'm seriously insane. If people fuck with me, I fuck with them back. I'll wreck their lives!"

She glanced over to see me grimace. "But not you. Don't worry baby girl," she grabbed my hands and peered into my eyes, "I'd never mess with you, no matter what. Even if we split up, I'd never hurt you."

I picked up her bong and took a puff of my own. Almost instantly I coughed. Vivian laughed. "Hey, I'm not used to these things!" I defended myself. "Let's move, we will be late."

Because of the ongoing bullying, Rosie was now in her new school. It was just a few blocks from our apartment. This time Rosie was going in as;

"Rosie." Nobody there would know that she used to be "Franklin." Vivian and I promised to meet her after school on her first day and walk her home.

"How did school go?" I asked.

"It was awesome! I love it here! Everyone is so nice!"

"That's wonderful!" I said. "But remember, it's only your first day, give it some time. No school is perfect."

Rosie nodded. "I lost a tooth!" she said, handing me a small box shaped like a treasure chest. "It's in there!"

"Really? I thought you finished losing teeth!" I teased her.

"I had to go to the office to get the box. The principal gave it to me. When I was in there, he kept calling me 'he' and saying 'him'. Another girl also lost her tooth, and she heard him do it."

"Aww crap!" I looked to Vivian. "You know, I met with her principal and counselor last week. They assured me this wouldn't be an issue! I was hoping for better communication! Last year was a nightmare."

"You don't let that principle call you 'he'!" Vivian said. "You tell him, 'don't mis-gender me!' Next time he calls you 'he' tell him, 'IM A GIRL!' Then if he does it again call him 'she'! See how he likes it!"

"I'll email your principal tonight, Rosie," I said. "I'll remind him to be careful. I doubt it's intentional, but he should be the one to set a good example. This all could be for nothing."

"I'll start a protest!" Vivian said. "I'll bring hundreds of trans girls to the school and we'll all have signs! We'll see if he mis-genders you after that!"

"I don't think that's necessary, Vivian. I think the email will be okay."

"Fuck that idiot principal! I'll get him fired! I'll get the school shut down, he's a prejudiced bitch!"

I wasn't sure if Vivian was serious, but her incessant ramblings mixed with the effects of the weed created the perfect combination for hilarity. I laughed so hard; I snorted.

"Listen to me, Rosie," Vivian was on a roll, "Be proud of who you are! I am proud to be transgender! If someone doesn't like it, then fuck them!"

"Yeah! Fuck them!" Rosie agreed.

"Rosie! Vivian! Language!" I scolded.

"You are fine the way you are, let nobody tell you any different! Trans pride! Trans pride!"

Okay, so maybe Vivian wasn't the best role model for Rosie, but as she was the only adult transgender woman we knew, she would have to do.

That night I sent the principal an email. He answered right away, denying the use of male pronouns to describe Rosie. Vivian's plan might not have been crazy after all.

Vivian helped me make dinner that evening while Rosie played outside with her friends. Vivian smoked more pot, and I polished off half a bottle of wine left over from the night before. Realizing we were out of garlic, I asked Vivian to run to the store for me. "Please go, I can't drive, I have been drinking. Plus, I have to keep an eye on Rosie and the stove!"

"Okay girl, I'll go. Let me take your car so I don't lose my parking spot."

"No problem," I said, giving her my keys, a twenty-dollar bill, and a kiss.

"I have to pick up a few things for myself, anyhow. Is that all you need?" she asked.

"Oh, and a $10 bottle of wine please, rosé! I'll text you some of my favorites!" Before she was out the door, I sent her six pictures of brands my local grocery store carried, which was why I was so disappointed when she came home with some cheap wine I hadn't heard of.

"Really," I asked, when she handed me the bottle. "Six brands to choose from weren't enough for you?"

"They had none of those," she lied. "I searched, this was all they had."

"Bullshit! I shop there practically every day!"

"Quit being such a wino, Five. Let me try it." I watched as she untwisted the top and took a swig from the bottle. After ingesting a large gulp she handed it back. "It's all right."

"Where's my change?" I asked.

"No change."

Defeated, and never one to waste alcohol, I poured myself a glass.

"Put that into a plastic cup. Let's go for a walk before dinner," Vivian said.

I knew by now that "walk" meant smoking a doobie in the park. I called Rosie in and fixed her a plate of food. She preferred the company of her cell phone and YouTube over a family dinner. "We'll be back in twenty minutes," I promised.

We headed to the park across the street. Vivian and I sat on a hidden bench that overlooked a miniature man-made lake. As we gazed out at the water, we took turns passing the joint. There was whispering coming from the dark path behind us, and we noticed a group of high school kids walking our way with their own lit joint.

"HEYYYYY BOYSSSS!" Vivian's voice reminded me of a wounded donkey. The air filled with roaring laughter, some of it my own. Within seconds the teenagers had high tailed it as far away from us as possible. I was off balance after the pot. We followed the trail home, and I curled my arm through Vivian's to steady myself.

"Will you help me?" I asked. But it was too late. Before I could spit out the last word, Vivian had let go of my arm and my foot struck a boulder. My body smashed onto the pavement with the force of a birthing hippo. I slid across the trail, my knees and elbows absorbing most of the blow. I smashed the wine cup and its contents spilled out, soaking my clothes.

"Ow!" I screamed.

"Whoa, what happened?" Vivian pulled me off the ground.

"I lost my balance and grabbed onto you! Why did you let go?"

"I had to adjust my arm."

Several streams of blood were trickling down my legs. The numbing from the booze wasn't much help. I hobbled the rest of the way home.

CHAPTER 14

Another week passed without Vivian, and I was dying for that bitch to get back from the carnival. It was her final day at the southern location. The next few weeks she was off while they moved it two hours north, to my neck of the woods. Two weeks off and six working locally? Why, I was about to be spending a couple months of quality time with my lengthy lady. Yippie! As luck would have it, it was also the one week a year Rosie spent at her dad's house. I couldn't wait to be alone with my six foot tall punk rock princess, and I was hoping we would spend part of that time naked! The only drawback was I sensed a cold coming on. I loaded up on Vitamin C, determined to keep it at bay.

My phone rang, "Hey Five!" It was my favorite voice on the other end of the line. "I'm on my way home!"

"Yay!" I said, followed by a cough.

"Are you getting sick, girl?" she asked.

"No! I won't let that happen, I want to be healthy for our alone time. This virus will not attack my body!"

"Aww. I can't wait to spend time with you too, Five! Listen girl, you won't believe this. I was on my lunch break, sitting next to two people who work at one of the carnival bars, and I overheard them saying they made over a grand in tips last night! Can you believe it?"

"Holy shit! No way! You should look into that," I said.

"Right? Brisket Billy's won't even allow us to take tips!"

"That's crazy."

"I mean, I am the best employee they have," she boasted. "I sell more than anybody else. Billy loves me, I make him the most money. I'm probably the best cashier he's ever hired."

"You are the best!"

"Hey, I think I may take a little road trip up north this week. I want to check out an amusement park I've never been to before. I can go for free with my Happy Hills season pass. You want to come with me?"

"I can't go, I have work, and the cats," I said.

"Well babe, I told you I take a road trip every year, and I have been planning to do this for a while. I just wasn't sure when."

I plopped down onto my couch. "But Rosie is gone for the week, and that only happens once a year. I was hoping we could spend some 'special time' together."

"I better hang up, gotta watch the road, we can talk when I get there."

"Okay. See you soon."

Despite my optimism, the virus had overtaken my body. I slept past Vivian's homecoming and almost through my alarm that next morning. Because I was so ill, I called out of work. Vivian was next to me holding my hand until a quarter past nine. I didn't even open my eyes as she arose from the bed. When the shower turned on, I fell back into my slumber knowing she would be in there a while. So when she kissed me goodbye in what seemed like only seconds later, it puzzled me.

"Where are you going?" I asked. Despite my attempt to ward it off, the illness was worsening and my throat was swelling. My body was hot and my cheeks flushed.

"To Berrywood, the amusement park, babe. Wow, you are burning up. You should try to get some sleep while I'm gone."

"Stay here," I said. "Take care of me."

"Hun, I've been working all week and I need to get out for a bit. Listen, I'll be back around 3:00 pm, okay? I'll bring you some soup. Rest!"

Even though I was disappointed she was leaving, she was right. I needed sleep. Besides, Berrywood was only thirty minutes away. At least this wasn't the road trip she kept talking about. Snoozing until she came home with some food was a wise idea, so I did.

It was already 4:00 pm when I awoke. The apartment was quiet and Vivian still wasn't back. I hadn't eaten since the day before and my tummy was grumbling. I picked up my phone and glanced at the screen. No new messages. Worried, I dialed her number. Halfway through the first ring, I heard the key turn in my door.

"Hey girl, how was the amusement park?" I asked.

"Awesome! Berrywood just opened a new roller coaster. It's insane, it has three loops!"

"Where's my soup?" The only thing in Vivian's hand was her purse.

"Huh?"

"You said you would bring me back some soup," I reminded her.

"Oh, they were all out," she lied. "How about we get some dinner?"

"I don't think I'm up for going anywhere."

"Order some takeout, I'll go pick it up," she offered.

I pondered her suggestion and realized there was only one thing that could make me feel better, booze. "I will get dressed. Let's try that little Italian place you keep mentioning."

The restaurant was empty. Other than a lone man at the bar, we were the only patrons. Still, the service was terrible. I ordered a glass of wine.

"Wow! You are going to drink when you are sick?"

"Shut up," I said.

It took the server twenty minutes to bring our refreshments. By the time we placed our order, we had memorized the menu. When the food arrived, it was cold. Vivian's chicken was floating on a plate of brown water, substituted for sauce. She sent it back and asked for spaghetti. The wait for my second glass of rose' took so long, I never caught a buzz. As we waited for the check, Vivian made a confession. "I'm leaving for my trip in the morning."

My jaw dropped onto the table.

"Seriously? Now? When I'm sick and when Rosie is gone?"

"You are welcome to come with me."

"You know I can't! This is terrible timing, Vivian. I need you this week. Can you please pick another time to go?"

"Are you telling me I can't?" she asked.

"No. I don't tell you what to do."

The server handed me the bill.

Once back at the apartment, Vivian packed for her lone adventure. "Do you think it's wise to be spending money on a vacation right now?" I asked. "I mean, you've been living here for three months and you haven't helped with the rent. I pay over $2000 a month before utilities…"

"I already told you, I won't be spending money on anything other than gas. I own a season pass for the parks and it includes my meals. I'll give you some cash for the water bill, I take long showers."

I climbed on my couch and curled into a ball. I couldn't stop the tears from falling. I was sick, helpless, and alone. After Vivian finished packing, she sat down next to me and turned on the TV. "Why don't you just go now?" I asked.

"Yeah, maybe I should."

My sarcasm was lost on her.

She reached over to give me a kiss, and I pulled away. Vivian shrugged. "I will get a head start to avoid traffic. I'm sorry you are crying, I hope you feel better." And just like that, she was gone.

Vivian called and texted the first two days, but I ignored her, and on the third day she stopped. The fourth day was torturous so on the fifth, I told her over text message to move out. She didn't respond. I waited for her to return on the sixth day as planned but she never arrived. I held strong through the seventh, but on the eighth day I broke. I messaged and begged her to come back home. Within two hours she was at my door and I had dinner waiting.

CHAPTER 15

Vivian was on her side, still comatose from the night before. She was wearing a tiny pair of hot pink panties and nothing else. Her long strawberry blonde hair lay curled on her pillow. I observed her breasts moving up and down each time she took a breath. I leaned in and caressed her closest nipple. Within seconds it was hard. I reached my other hand to the front of her silky panties to find that her 'clit' was hard too. Softly, I slid them to her knees and placed my face against her crotch. I circled the head of her 'clit' with my tongue until I felt it throbbing. I took it in my mouth and sucked. Minutes later she was on top of me.

"Hey Five, Rising Fly is playing next month in our town!" Vivian's voice startled me awake. I must have fallen back asleep after my orgasm.

"Oh shit! I love them! I've wanted to experience them live for over a decade," I said, now wide awake. Vivian and I were in my bed on a Sunday morning. I was off, and she didn't have to be at work that day until noon. She was holding my arm with her right hand and scrolling through her phone with her left. "Tickets are only $25."

"Get them!" I said.

"I would, babe, but I'm broke until payday."

"Buy them anyway. Use my credit card!" I said, pointing to my wallet on the dresser.

"They want $19 apiece on top of the ticket price for processing fees!"

"That's okay. They are still cheap."

"No way are we paying that! I'm going there to buy them. Do you want to come with me? Come on, babe!"

"Seriously? But I want to be lazy today," I said, nibbling on her ear. "We can go for round two."

"You know I'd love to, but my hormones lowered my sex drive."

"It's fine, hun. I've had more sex with you than in any other relationship. I don't think I could handle you if you weren't taking hormones," I teased.

"Will you go with me?"

"Okay! Fine! But I'm taking a 'roadie'." I went into the kitchen to pour myself a lidded cup of wine.

The two of us spent an hour together doing our makeup and giggling like we were in junior high. Vivian pulled out her electric razor and shaved her face. "You don't know how lucky you are, not having facial hair, it's excruciating!"

"I shave my face!" I admitted.

"You do?"

"Totally. I've got a pesky chin hair and lots of peach fuzz on my cheeks!"

"It's not the same thing!" she said, rolling her eyes.

"How much is laser hair removal?"

"It's not that expensive. I bought a six-pack of sessions on sale once."

"What was the name of the clinic?"

Vivian looked it up on her phone and I searched the company on Groupon. The sale she mentioned was still going, so I ordered them for her as a gift, "Check your email! I got you something."

"Aww thanks, babe!"

"Book your first session!"

"No, I better wait until I have time off work. I need to let my facial hair grow out for a few days first, I hate looking like a man."

I watched Vivian slip on a spaghetti-strapped dress. I chose a strapless one and a pair of rhinestone encrusted flip flops.

"Do you know where the venue is?" I asked. We had just buckled into Vivian's car. "Yeah, basically."

"Should I map it?"

"No," she said.

Although it was only four miles from my apartment, the area was hard to access and Vivian was driving in circles. When she wasn't paying attention, I pulled up a map. "We can't go this way Vivian. There isn't access."

"Yes, we can. It's right there, look!" Vivian drove across a dirt road that led to a military base. In the far distance, I could see the outline of the building we were trying to get to.

"Come on Vivian, it's another dead end! The map says we should merge onto the freeway and go around the back." My suggestions were unheard; I figured I had better get tough. "Well Vivian, ladies stop and ask for directions. When you wander around like this, you are acting like a man."

Vivian was still ignoring me. In the distance I could make out the uniforms of armed policemen. They were standing in front of a long barbed wire fence and one of them had the leash of a gigantic German shepherd in his hand. Remembering the roadie I had in the console, and the joints stashed in Vivian's glove box, I was sure we were going to prison. Vivian pulled up next to them and rolled down her window. "I'm trying to find the music venue that's on this street."

"You can not come through here without clearance, you need to turn back," an officer said. "Go back the way you came in. You will make a loop and then a direct left." Luckily, the police didn't search her vehicle. After a million years, we made it.

"Two tickets to Rising Fly please." The attendant handed Vivian the seating chart. "How much are these?" she asked him, pointing to a row in the far back.

"$22."

"Ask him how much for the floor!" I interrupted.

"How much is the general admission to the floor?"

"$75."

"Oh, my God, get the floor! Get floor!" I was so excited.

Back at the apartment, my lady lumps stuck the tickets to the fridge with a magnet next to the baseball ones she had bought for Rosie.

"Wow, some big dates are coming up, do you think we will still be together by then?" I asked.

"Of course! Why wouldn't we be?" Vivian looked at me like I was insane.

I planted myself at the kitchen table and noticed Rosie's phone plugged into the wall. She was at her dad's house for the weekend and I hadn't heard from her, which was unusual. Now I knew why, she forgot it. I had been neglecting my parental duties and unlocked it to take a peek. I should have been keeping a closer eye on her internet activity. After a quick scroll through her search engine, I glanced through her open windows and I shrieked when I saw it!

"What?" Vivian asked.

"HOLY SHIT!"

"What? What?" she asked again.

"I can't, oh, my God. I just can't..." I handed Vivian the phone, not being able to put words to what I saw.

"That little bitch!" Vivian shouted.

"What's wrong with her? She needs to go back to counseling! She's sick! Twisted! Did you know she did this?" I asked. "Did you see it happen?"

"Hell no! I don't understand when she could have done it. If I saw her there, I would have flipped out!"

She handed me back the phone and without a second look; I deleted the photo that Rosie had taken of Vivian and I having sex.

CHAPTER 16

V ivian had an insatiable obsession with roller coasters, so it didn't take her long to persuade me to join her for a day at Happy Hills. Pulling into the parking lot of a liquor store she began her manipulation. "Come on Asterisk, let's go get a bottle of tequila. I'll drink with you tomorrow at the amusement park, it will be fun! I know where there is an amazing frozen lemonade stand. We can use that as the mixer." Tequila and frozen lemonade? That bitch had twisted my arm.

The sun hadn't yet risen the next morning when Vivian pushed me awake. "Come on Five! Get up, we have to get going if we are planning to beat traffic."

"What? No way! It's too early!"

"Come on, Mommy! Get dressed," Rosie said.

"You have her up already too?"

"Yes! Now lets get out of here."

I threw on some makeup and a sundress, then walked into the kitchen and filled a small cooler with ice and the unopened bottle of tequila. I grabbed Vivian's refillable Happy Hills cups, and we were off. Traffic was bumper to bumper, but I didn't care. Vivian was driving, and she had a hold of my hand the entire time. I leaned into my luscious lady friend and felt all gushy being there beside her. About two hours later we finally arrived at the park. I opened the car door and stepped out. The hot air hit me like a ton of bricks. It was mid-July, and we were in the middle of a heat wave. I looked at Vivian's dash to read the thermometer, 108° and it was still morning. Great. I headed to the back of Vivian's car, popped the trunk, and filled our cups with tequila.

"Hurry!" Vivian said. "I want to be the first through the gate!"

"I'm almost done, one second."

"Your priorities are screwed up, Asterisk. One of the security guards might see you."

"Well, come and block me then!"

Vivian came around from behind, and I handed her a cup to hold. She grabbed it halfheartedly and began a conversation with Rosie. Before I knew it, she had sat it down and it spilled.

"God damn it, Vivian!" I yelled.

"What? Come on Asterisk, my car will stink like liquor!"

"I asked you to hold it! Ugh! Never mind. Let's go in."

As we were approaching the gate, Vivian leaned into me and whispered, "I only have one free friends ticket. But I have my ex's and her little sister's season passes on my phone. I don't think you could pass for my ex but I bet I can get Rosie in as her little sister. The only problem is they scan your fingerprints."

"Yeah, that sounds like a bad idea," I said to Vivian. "I'll just buy Rosie's ticket, it's not a big deal."

"No! This will work!" Vivian said. "Rosie, your name is 'Patty' today, all right?"

Rosie didn't understand, and I was a little ashamed to be teaching such an immoral lesson to my kid. But I was also eager to get inside and fix myself a frozen cocktail, so I played along.

I was the first one through ticketing, then it was Rosie's turn. Her fingerprint didn't match. Obviously.

"I don't think that's the right pass," the young girl working the gate concluded. She attempted to match the fingerprint several times.

"Here! Try mine!" Vivian said. They accepted hers.

"Wait a second, why do you have mine under my old name?" she asked.

"It says 'Johnathan'."

"'Johnathan' is my 'dead name'! I am a lady! It should be under the name 'Vivian'! I complain every time I come here. Why won't you guys change it for me? I don't understand why I can't get it fixed! You are all prejudiced!" Vivian leaned over into the crowded line next to us and yelled, "Happy Hills hates transgender people!"

I understood the scene wasn't about saving a few bucks; it was about Vivian seeing what she could get away with. I had two open containers in my hands making me nervous. Lucky for me the girl at the gate was feeling pressured and decided just to usher us over to customer relations. Once to the window, Vivian started in on her name change and made everyone working the booth so uncomfortable, they forgot about Rosie's entrance fee.

"Isn't that stealing?" Rosie asked.

Fuck.

"Yes, it is. We are setting a bad example for you, and I'm sorry."

"There's the lemonade stand," Vivian said. "One frozen lemonade, please!" she ordered from the boy at the window.

"I don't think that will be enough. Why don't you order two?" I asked.

"One will be fine." Vivian grabbed the slushy and walked away. I handed the cashier a handful of single dollar bills and didn't bother to wait for the change. Vivian and Rosie were already about fifteen feet ahead of me. I scurried to catch up.

"Stop!" I yelled. "Stop right here!" I pointed to a picnic bench, and we formed a circle around it. "Hand me the lemonade so I can mix the drinks," I said. Instead Vivian grabbed the cups from my hand and did the mixing herself, spilling frozen lemonade everywhere. Just as I had thought, there wasn't enough to mix with the tequila. I voiced my complaint and Vivian brushed it off.

"We can stop and fill up a cup with some free lemonade from the soda fountain later. Let's go, I want to be first in line for my favorite coaster!"

Rosie and I followed Vivian to her favorite ride. I knew Rosie wouldn't get on. Roller coasters frightened her, and this one was gigantic. Instead, she waited by the side while we rode it without her. We did another two rides this way, and I was feeling too guilty to continue. "Vivian, I will take Rosie over to the kid's area and catch up with you later."

"No way, girl! I don't want to ride alone. Quit being such a baby, Rosie. Kids much smaller than you ride these coasters all the time."

"That's true, Rosie. You should at least try one. You are almost as tall as I am. They may not let you on the children's rides anymore."

The three of us ventured over to the kiddie area anyway. Another little girl close to Rosie's age was going on rides alone. They quickly made friends. I decided it would be okay for Rosie to stay there with her friend as long as she checked in every hour.

Now that Rosie was having a good time, I could relax and enjoy some of my tequila. It went down a lot easier after being filled with lemonade from the fountain. Less than an hour later, our cups were empty.

"Have you been on this before?" Vivian asked, pointing to a roller coaster that had its riders on their stomachs.

"No, I haven't. Let's do it."

The line was long and Vivian passed the time by making friends with the people behind us. One miniature man seemed to have an infatuation with Vivian, I don't think he even reached five foot. He was wearing a blue, red and pink tie-dyed shirt and a matching bandanna. His pupils had dilated, and he was apparently high on something other than life. Vivian didn't seem to notice or if she did, she didn't mind. She was excited to be connecting with someone over punk rock. After a while, she grew bored and turned back to converse with me. That's when I realized her little friend had vanished.

"Where did your buddy go?"

"I don't know. His friends are still waiting, he must have gone to the bathroom or something."

The line was moving again, and it was nearing our turn to ride. That's when it happened. All I could see was a blur of tie dye pummeling towards us.

BOOM!

Faster than a bird could get sucked into the propeller of an airplane, the little man came pelting through the crowd and catapulted his body into Vivian! The blunt force knocked her off her platforms and across the divide, before flying into a tree. Just as fast as he had thrown her, a group of men from the line pulled her from the dirt. Covered in mud and thorns, she resumed her place. She would not miss her turn on the coaster over this. Despite the pain, she was laughing. "That was the craziest thing that's ever happened to me!"

"Vivian, you are bleeding! Turn around."

As she rotated her body, I could see her shirt had torn in several places and she had bloody scratches on her back and neck.

"Oh my goodness, babe. I didn't see that coming or I would have tried to stop it."

"Where did the little guy go now?" she asked. Like Houdini, he had disappeared. The line moved once more, and it was our turn to ride the attraction. As we approached our seats, Vivian's tiny friend stole mine. I shook my head and gave up, exiting the ride. Vivian took a seat next to him. As the coaster took off, I saw him grab her hand. After it ended, Vivian joined me at the exit while baby Houdini pulled off another one of his famous disappearing acts.

"That was nuts!" Vivian said.

"What happened?" I asked, hoping there wasn't much more she could add to the story.

"He grabbed my hand and squeezed it so hard, I thought he would break it, and he didn't let go the entire ride. Then he confessed that he wants to be trans."

"You think he was serious, or just high?" I asked her.

"I don't know, but it was nuts!"

We made our way into a gift shop and Vivian bought herself a pink, fitted baby-T. "My cleavage looks so good in this!"

"And you have a waistline. See, I told you. Girls shouldn't wear T-shirts!"

"Ugh. I'm punk rock, Asterisk. I like my band shirts!"

I just shook my head. "Let's go get some lunch, I'm starving. Is there somewhere to eat inside? I need a break from this heat."

On our way to the park's restaurant, we stopped off and grabbed Rosie from the kiddie area. Once inside the eatery, the hostess greeted us. "It will be a ten-minute wait."

That wasn't an issue for me. I was just glad to be out of the extreme weather and somewhere cool. I took a seat in their waiting area and the next thing I knew I was on the floor. Rosie and Vivian were both laughing. My face turned red. I wasn't sure if it was the effects of the tequila or the overexposure to heat that had caused me to slip off the chair, but I wasn't doing well. I decided some food and a cold beer would be the answer. Lucky for me, even though I had fallen, the restaurant served me anyway.

After lunch, Rosie headed back to the kids rides to catch up with her new friend while I accompanied Vivian on more roller coasters. We were in line for one I hadn't been on yet when the attendant motioned us to stop. "Wait right there!" Vivian didn't like this one bit. "Why are you stopping us! I want to go on the ride right now!"

"This car is full, Sir. You can go on the next one. It will be here in just a moment."

Uh oh!

"What did you just call me? I AM NOT A SIR! I am a woman! Can't you see that? This entire place is full of haters! HAPPY HILLS HATES TRANSGENDER PEOPLE!"

"Shh! It's okay," I said to her in a whisper. "We will get on the next one. Just chill out."

"I don't want to go on the next one! I want to go on this one!" Vivian pouted like a preschooler. "This bitch won't let me on because she hates trans people!" Suddenly the floodgate of tears had opened, and Vivian's eyes produced more water than the log ride. "Everyone working here is prejudice!"

"I'm so sorry," I mouthed to the attendant. "Come on, Vivian." I ushered her out of the line. "Let's go to the car and smoke a joint!" Apparently those were the magic words because the bitch followed me. After hot boxing the car, Vivian was back to her cheery old self. We made our way back into the park and scooped up Rosie just as the sun was going down.

Although Vivian was now full of life, I felt deflated. My blood pressure was rising, and the temperature had finally taken its toll on my body. "I think I'm ready to head back."

"What? Already? No way! The park doesn't close until ten!"

"Yeah, but we have been here all day, and I'm tired. I really need to rest."

"You are being selfish, Asterisk! Rosie hasn't even gone on a roller coaster yet and she promised she would go on one now. Don't you want your child to experience a giant coaster for the first time?"

"Rosie had all day to go on whatever she wanted. It's late now. She has to go to school in the morning. Please, can we just head out?" I begged.

"We are not leaving this early. Quit being a baby! Rosie and I are going on this coaster! You can join us or you can wait on that bench."

The line for the ride was forty minutes long, so I chose the bench. I sat alone and waited. When I saw them exiting the ride, I let out a sigh of relief.

"I loved it! I wasn't even scared! We are going on again, Mommy!" Rosie said.

"No, no, no. I'm ready to leave," I reminded them.

"Wow!" Vivian stepped in. "You didn't even tell Rosie how proud you were she went on her first coaster. Now she wants to ride it again and you don't want her to? I'm sorry you have to have a mom like that Rosie. Don't take it to heart. She should be proud of your accomplishment!"

I wanted to smack her. "Please, can we just go?"

"After we ride it one more time. You should come with us."

"I feel like I might pass out."

"You are so full of shit!" Vivian's words trailed off as she and Rosie made their way back to the line.

Even though I was half melted to the bench I survived. By the time we made it back to the car it was a quarter to ten. We didn't make it home until after midnight, and I had to call Rosie out sick the next day.

CHAPTER 17

It was a Saturday evening in early August. Vivian was working for Brisket Billy's at the carnival again, only this time the carnival was just a short car ride away! "Come meet me at the fair tonight, I will get you girls in for free and give you food if you visit my stand!" Vivian promised.

"Rosie will love that, but I don't care about the food, I want those giant beers! If I take an Uber there will you bring us back when you get off?"

"Of course, hun!"

I arrived home from work with Rosie late that afternoon. As promised, Vivian had left us two free admission tickets stuck to the front of the refrigerator. I popped open a beer, changed my clothes and ordered us a ride. Although it only took about ten minutes to get there, the lines leading in were insane and stretched half a city block. By the time we made it through the gates, it was dark out and my bladder was ready to explode. Our first stop was the bathroom. Yippee, there was a line there too!

On our way to find Vivian's food stand we stopped, and I ordered a $25 gallon-sized IPA. Hooray!

Once we located Vivian's booth, we stepped into her line and waited for service. She hadn't spotted us yet. Even though she was wearing her "Vivian" name tag, she looked mostly male. Her long hair was hidden behind a baseball cap and she had on her ugly board shorts again. Above it was a T-shirt with the Brisket Billy's logo on it that ultimately engulfed any traces of mammary glands. The only thing making her look remotely female was the shimmery polish I had brushed on her fingertips the night before.

Her eyes lit up a tiny bit when she noticed us. But true to her game she pretended that she didn't know who we were so she could smuggle us an irrational amount of carnival concessions. "Go wait at the end of the counter!" She instructed us as if we were actual paying customers.

A moment later Vivian was back with four gigantic trays of fried grub. Rosie's eyes about popped out of her skull upon seeing them. "Hang on, there's more." It was already too much, but she continued. I realized we had to carry the entirety to a table ourselves. "Let me see your arms Rosie," I loaded them full of as many goodies as she could carry. We had fried lobster, steak, brisket (of course), Twinkies, pineapples, Oreos, the list goes on. We looked like two obese billionaires carrying all that food through the carnival. Each item cost around $20 a piece!

When we finally found a place to sit, I arranged our feast around us. It was ridiculous. We ate until we wanted to barf but barely made a dent in it. I felt horrible throwing it into the trash.

"Do you want to go on rides?" I asked Rosie.

"No, I want to play games, can we? Please?"

"Sure!"

That little turd had her mind set to play the ring toss game that gave out the goldfish as prizes. "Every one is a winner!" the game attendant shouted.

I was about to gain the burden of carrying around a live fish for the next three hours. Great. The worker handed me the living prize. "No Mommy, I want to carry him!" Rosie said.

I pondered it for a second, "Okay, but only if you are careful. No splashing around, you need to keep the tank steady!"

"I will, I promise!"

My negative mood quickly swung in the polar opposite direction when something grabbed my waist and pushed me into a wall. It was Vivian, and before I could mumble a word, she had her tongue in my mouth. Aww, how I loved her.

"I'm on break, babe!"

"Yay! Thanks for the food, it was too much though!"

"I told you I would hook you guys up!" she said proudly. "Didn't I tell you I would hook you up, Rosie?"

My daughter nodded.

"That was nice, but I don't want to get you in trouble at work," I said.

"Billy loves me! I'll never get in trouble. Besides, they don't keep inventory. Do you know how much food they throw away at the end of the night? A lot! Besides, I make Billy tons of money. I'm his best employee!" she assured me. I had heard that line before.

"Okay. Just don't get caught."

"Have you petted the farm animals yet?" Vivian asked Rosie.

"No! Not yet!"

"Where are they?" I asked, "I couldn't find them."

"I'll take you!"

We followed Vivian to the petting zoo. Rosie was having a hard time being gentle with her fish. Noticing half the water had already splashed out I took it from her. The novelty had ran out by then and she was more intrigued by the goats, so she let it go with little fight. Soon, Vivian's break ended. I helped myself to another beer and bought Rosie an ice cream. As the night progressed we headed over to the main stage to watch the band play. Before it ended, Vivian had found us again.

"I got off early, baby girl," she said, grabbing my hand. "Come on, I want to take you to my favorite spot." Vivian led us over to a beautiful flower garden. "This is where I hang out when I call you on my breaks." Aww, she was so cute.

"We should stop off and smoke a joint on the way home. I know a little park close to here. Rosie can play on the swings. Are you down?" The mega beers had done their job, so I was fine with just about anything. "Sure."

It was a long hike back to the car. Vivian kept hold of my hand as I walked to her left with Rosie in front of us. My manipulative child had convinced me to let her try carrying the goldfish again. This time she seemed more responsible. Two men were heading down the sidewalk in our direction when it happened.

BAM!

Vivian intentionally slammed her shoulder into the man closest to her.

"What the fuck?" he called out.

Vivian was looking for a fight. "Please, don't," I begged. "Not in front of Rosie."

Vivian ignored me. "I'm trying to walk with my girl! What? Do you expect me to push her off the curb? You better show me some respect!"

Luckily the man was more mature than my partner. He shook it off and kept going.

A lifetime later we made it to the car. I took the goldfish from Rosie while we drove. I was looking forward to stopping for the doobie because I knew it would relieve Vivian's rage. The second we had stopped in front of the park, Rosie started up about the fish again. "Please, can I have him now?"

"Fine, set him on the floor, all right?" I handed it over the seat. When I saw that Rosie had a firm grip on it, I let go, and opened the car door to step out.

"Uh oh!" she said.

"Uh oh, what?"

"I spilled it."

I let out a sigh. "You spilled how much?"

"You better not be getting nasty fish water in my car!" Vivian yelled.

"I spilled all of it."

"What do you mean 'all of it'?" I asked. I looked into the back seat to see the tank was empty and the fish was flopping around on the floor. "Oh my God! Vivian! Do you have a bottle of water in the car? The fish needs water! He will die!"

"Nope, I don't," she said.

I ran around the vehicle to the back where Rosie was sitting, grabbed the fish and put it into it's empty tank. "Open your trunk Vivian! Rosie, look under the seat! There has to be a bottle of water in here somewhere!" But there wasn't. Desperate to save the damn thing, I scanned my surroundings. In the distance, I could see a broken sprinkler flooding a small area. Terrarium in hand, I hauled ass in its direction. I used my palm to direct the cold water into it. Once there was enough to support the fish, I returned it to the car. My clothes and hair were sopping wet, and I was shivering. I hadn't noticed in my emergency, but Rosie was already at the playground swinging and Vivian was sitting on a patch of grass atop a small hill smoking weed without me. I left the fish in the car and joined Vivian on the hill.

"Can we just leave, I want to get this fish into some better water before it dies. Who knows what this reclaimed water may have in it. Plenty of chemicals, I'm sure."

"Why bother?" Vivian asked. "It's gonna die, anyway. Carnival fish always die."

"That's because people don't know how to take care of them! I have had lots of fish and..."

"You are ruining the night over a stupid fish, Asterisk. Here," she said, handing me the lit joint.

"I'm sorry. I'll try to have fun," I said, taking a hit and then passing it back. I sat for a few minutes and did my best to move on, but all I could think about was the damn fish. "Look I can't enjoy myself when there is an animal suffering. Can we just finish smoking this at home? It's getting late and Rosie should be in bed."

I watched as Vivian threw the pot down the hill. "Forget it. You can't relight a joint, they taste like shit that way. Besides, you already killed the vibe."

We drove back home in silence. Once Rosie was in her room, I opened a beer and tried handing it to Vivian. "I don't want that shit. I'm going to bed. I don't know why you have to drink so damn much anyway. You aren't a lonely single mom anymore. You have me!" she said.

"Hey! I'm not with you because I'm lonely! I'm perfectly content being single. You are here because I want you here, don't forget that!" I took a breath. "Though, I might not be so sure, now that I know you lack empathy!"

Vivian let out a chuckle, "Yeah, whatever you have to tell yourself."

She went into the bedroom, crawled into my bed and pulled a blanket over her body.

The next morning Rosie found her fish floating upside down in its tank.

CHAPTER 18

I arrived home from work that evening to a surprise. "Hey Five!" my girlfriend greeted me, "I made you vomit!" I wasn't feeling sick, so I didn't understand what she was talking about. "For dinner! I made vomit! It's my own culinary creation! Here," she said, handing me a giant bowl of food which in fact resembled throw-up.

"That looks... appealing."

"Try it! You'll love it!" she promised. Upon further inspection I could see it was some kind of meat and vegetable scooped over potatoes. It reminded me of an upside down Shepard's pie. I took a bite. She was right; it was delicious. "What about yours?" I asked, sitting down to the table with my giant bowl of stoner food.

"Rosie and I already ate."

"You didn't wait for me?" I let out a sigh.

"Why would we? We were hungry! Plus, I have to get ready. I'm going to the trans club tonight with my girls. Are you cool with that? I haven't seen them in a while."

"Oh, yeah. I don't care," I said between bites.

Vivian's giant blue eyes lit up, "You should come with me!"

"I can't. I have work in the morning."

"Oh, come on, it would be so hot to have you there. Men go to the clubs to hit on trans girls, having you around to make out with would confuse them. It would be hilarious to watch. Please?"

"Maybe some other time, if we plan it first. I will take the following day off work and get Rosie a babysitter." I hadn't been out to a club in over a decade, and to be honest, I felt too old for it back then.

"Rosie, you should come!" Vivian said. "You want to hang out with some trans girls? You don't know any trans girls other than me, do you?"

"Really, Vivian? You can't take a child to a nightclub! What are you thinking?"

Rosie was standing by the front door with the old plastic terrarium from her dead fish in her hand, "Mom, can I go catch a lizard?"

"Sure, but you can't keep it. You must let it out before you go to bed tonight."

Vivian interrupted, "Why would you want to catch a lizard, Rosie? That's what boys do! You are such a little boy aren't you? You aren't really trans!"

Rosie looked like she was about to cry.

"Vivian! Stop it! Rosie is a girl too," I said.

"No, she's not! She isn't even taking hormones yet." Vivian looked to Rosie, "Until you take female hormones you are just a cross dresser, a little boy in girl's clothes."

I had heard enough. "You are a fucking hypocrite, Vivian! If someone called you a boy, you would go nuts! I used to catch lizards and frogs and snakes when I was a kid, does that make me a fucking boy? You better knock this shit off right now and apologize to her!"

Vivian chuckled. "Aww, Rosie did I hurt your feelings?"

"Apologize!"

"Rosie, I'm sorry if I hurt your feelings," she said, making her way into the bathroom. As usual, she left the door slightly ajar.

I walked into the kitchen to rinse out my bowl when I noticed it. Someone had left the gas burner on low. It hit me; I wasn't the one who took the food off the stove a few weeks back. It was Vivian. I was still outside smoking that night when she made her plate. Pissed, I turned it off and spun around to confront her.

Before I could enter the restroom, something interrupted me. Standing by the crack in the door was Rosie. She was yet again peeking inside to see Vivian in the nude. She had already done enough creepy shit to last a lifetime! My blood was boiling. "Do you want to see Vivian naked? Just ask her, I'm sure she will show you!" Rosie's eyes widened.

Vivian, upon hearing the commotion, chimed in. "You want to see my boobies, Rosie? I'll show you."

"No, thanks!" Rosie screamed, and bolted out the front door.

Vivian and I were in hysterics.

Once we calmed down, Vivian started the water for her shower. Rosie wouldn't dare come back for a while, and I'd already forgotten about the stove. So I sneaked into the bathroom, slipped off my dress and climbed in with Vivian. "What are you doing, girl?" she asked.

"I wanted to give you a little something before you go," I teased.

"I'm kind of in a hurry."

"I'll be quick."

I slid my nails down the back of Vivian's neck as I pressed her breasts against mine. I could feel her getting hard as I kissed her so I reached down and took her 'clit' into my hand. I stroked it while warm water ran over our bodies. It only took a few minutes for her to orgasm. "What about you?" she asked.

"You can get me back later tonight." I winked.

I hopped out and dried myself off. Seconds after my exit, the loogies began. After what seemed like eons, my little tranny phlegm factory finally turned off the water. As usual, she transformed my kitchen table into her personal vanity. We talked for over an hour while she detailed her face. When she finished, she looked like a cross between Elvira and Tammy Faye Bakker.

I gave her look a once-over. "You want your bottom eyeliner like that?"

"Why? What's wrong with it?"

"It's just so thick. You can go heavy on the upper lid, but on the bottom, it looks outdated."

"I'm punk rock!" she said. I didn't get what being punk rock had to do with fucked up eyeliner, but I let it go.

Vivian slipped into a pair of black tights and a loose knee-length skirt. She pulled a padded bra over her chest but then hid her breasts inside an over-sized T-shirt. I spoke up again. "That doesn't go together, if you must wear the T-shirt, pair it with some fishnets and a short leather skirt. Or, if you want to go with the long skirt... No actually, you are going to a club, ditch the long skirt!"

"I like what I am wearing!" she said, giving me her usual prepubescent sounding attitude. She shoved her hooves into a velvety pair of six-inch platforms and waddled over to where I was laying. She gave me a kiss on the mouth that left a ring of black lipstick on my face. "I'll be home later tonight. I'm gonna jump on you, then I'm gonna fuck you while I'm dressed up all cute." She blew me another kiss as she slid out the door.

Vivian didn't make it back until after the sun had come up the next morning. I was already in the kitchen making Rosie's breakfast. She headed straight into the bathroom to wash her makeup off, then plopped down onto my bed without so much as a hello. Within seconds she was out like a light.

CHAPTER 19

The sound of Vivian's cell phone awakened me. She rejected the call. As I dozed back off, it rang a second time. Again she denied the call. It rang once more only this time she answered.

"What the hell Vivian? Who's calling you this early?" I asked.

"It's Peter! He's always doing this, he doesn't understand that everybody in the world doesn't keep his nine-to-five hours."

I peered at the clock; it was only 7:00 am.

"What do you want Peter?" Vivian screamed into her phone. She was wide awake now! Her voice sounded like an angry wrestler. "What the fuck, dude?"

CLICK!

She hung up on her friend. The phone rang again. This time she answered in her 'lady' voice. "Hey sweetheart, how's your morning going, honnn-ney?"

I could hear Peter on the other end, "You aren't a girl, dude. You are a guy. I have known you your entire life."

"What sugar? You think I'm a guy? No, baby, I'm a hot lady. You want a piece of this? I know you think I'm sexy?" she chuckled.

"Fuck you, dude!"

"You want to fuck me?" Vivian asked.

This time Peter hung up. Vivian scrolled the internet on her phone.

"Why do you put up with that treatment?" I asked her.

"That's just how Peter is."

"That doesn't make his abuse acceptable! Look at Rosie for example. I grew her in my body, birthed her, named her 'Franklin', yet I still have no issue calling her by the correct pronouns and the name she picked out. If I can do it, everyone else in the world can. You should really ditch that prick. His friendship isn't worth it."

"We've known each other since we were kids. Peter is just... Peter." Vivian changed the subject. "Happy Hills season passes go on sale next weekend! It's the best bargain of the year. That's when I buy mine."

Realizing she was attempting to manipulate me into ordering them for Rosie and myself, I called her out on it. "I thought you were buying us the passes? I didn't even want them. I bought Barrywood passes last year and I couldn't get Rosie to go more than once. It was a total waste of money."

"Aww, come on Five. We will have so much fun! I want to buy them for you guys but I can't at the moment and the sale only lasts a few days. If you don't order them now, they will double in price. Anyway, I can't afford to, I don't even know what I will do about my car insurance. It's due tomorrow and I don't get paid until next week."

"Do you want me to add your car onto my policy?" I asked.

"Yes, please. I'll pay you back on payday, I promise. Thanks Five."

I would not let Vivian manipulate me into buying season passes to Happy Hills, but I realized her car insurance was a priority. Besides, she did most of the driving around while I drank; I knew I couldn't let there be a lapse and lose my designated driver. I picked up my cell and made a quick call to my insurance agent. "He will email me the paperwork. We can send it over in the morning."

Out of the blue, Vivian let out a blood-curdling shriek.

"Ahhhh! Oh my God! Roach! There's a cockroach!"

Faster than I could let out a fart, Vivian had thrown her hands in the air and ran out of my bedroom. "Get it, hun! Oh, my God! Get it, Rosie!" she pleaded.

I lunged for my shoe. Rosie ran into the bathroom, searching for the bug spray. Before either of us stopped it, my cat picked up the bug in her mouth and headed towards Vivian.

"Ahh! That cats possessed!"

"She's bringing you a present," I giggled.

"Fuck that cat! I hate cats!" The truth had just come out.

We all watched helplessly as the cat scurried through a small opening in Vivian's closet door with the half-chewed insect still dangling from her teeth. It seemed like this was Vivian's karma for being so mean to her. A few seconds later, the cat exited the closet empty-mouthed.

"You think she ate it, or left it in there?" I asked.

Vivian carefully opened the door the rest of the way. All that was visible was a pile of wrinkled clothes, shoes and bottles of hormone pills.

"If you kept your things organized, we might be able to find it," I said.

Vivian let out a sigh of defeat. "You want to get ready to go, or what? We might have a little extra time before the game. I want to take you to my favorite brewery down the street." It was a Sunday afternoon and as luck would have it, Vivian and I hadn't broken up yet! That's right, we were heading out to the baseball game Vivian bought tickets for a month prior.

Vivian, Rosie and I loaded into Vivian's car and headed to the stadium. Once parked in the adjacent lot, we followed Vivian down a long side street to a hidden brewery. It was heaven! I ordered a beer flavored with chocolate while Vivian's had a hint of banana. After a short taste test, we realized that we liked each other's better and swapped. There wasn't much for Rosie to do, and she fidgeted, so I suggested we head back to the stadium. We still had an hour to kill.

I passive-aggressively nagged Vivian about the early morning phone call. "It looks like we still have a while until the game starts. Too bad we couldn't have slept in."

"Girl, chill out! I have a plan. Come on."

After downing the rest of our beers, Vivian led us back to the parking garage and through a dark corridor that exited outside. We stepped into a hidden grassy nook inside a wooden fence.

"What do you think?" she asked.

"Think of what?"

"Our secret smoking spot!" she said. I watched her reach into her purse and pull out a joint and lighter. Within seconds it was lit.

"Hey Mommy, what's that?" Rosie asked, pointing to a half-dead tree.

"You don't know what a tree is?" Vivian taunted.

"No, that!" Rosie was referring to a used syringe someone had discarded in the tree's bend.

"Oh, for fuck's sake, Vivian! Let's get out of here."

"In a minute," she said, passing me the joint.

I took a puff. "People use those to take drugs," I told my tween. I released a cloud of smoke. "Never do drugs. They will kill you!"

"Uh, aren't you doing drugs now, Mommy?" she asked. Gulp. Once again I felt like a piece of shit, doing another thing in front of her I wasn't proud of.

"Marijuana isn't a real drug, honey. It's legal like alcohol or cigarettes."

Rosie shook. "So you will die of cancer!"

"No, no, honey. Not like cigarettes in that way. I'm just going to act stupid for an hour and I could get into trouble if I drove a car."

"Good thing Vivian is driving," she said.

"Yes, a good thing. But we aren't leaving for a long time and this will wear off by then."

"It stinks." she said.

Vivian and I giggled.

"Finish it Vivian, let's go." I headed to the exit.

"I'm hungry," Rosie said.

"Do you want ice cream?" Vivian asked.

"Yes!"

"How about some nachos? They have the best nachos here!"

We made our way into the stadium, and over to concessions and, as promised, I treated Rosie to her ice cream and nachos. We stopped at the bar and I purchased two of the biggest beers I had ever seen. Treats in hand, we wandered around until we found our seats. We were on the top level of the stadium and the players resembled a trail of ants. I didn't care; I was just there to drink. Rosie grew bored, so we wandered around the stadium a while more, splurging on peanuts, cotton candy and several rounds of beer. We didn't stay for the entire game. At least, I didn't remember if we had.

The next thing I knew, it was 8:00 pm. Vivian was resting beside me and playing on her phone when I opened my eyes. My mouth felt like a desert and everything looked blurry. I reached over and touched Vivian's thigh. She pushed my hand away.

"Ew! Don't! You are gross!"

"Why? What did I do?" I asked.

"You don't remember? Yah, okay."

"I don't!"

"You were too fucking drunk. Why do you do that to yourself, girl?"

"What?"

"After we got home, you dropped on the ground by the front patio. The door was wide open. You pulled up your dress and tried to get me to fuck you! It was so gross! You were acting like a dude."

I let out an embarrassed giggle, "Aww, I'm sorry. Come here."

Vivian rolled into a corner. "Ew! No! You gross me out! It will be a long time before I'll let you touch me again."

CHAPTER 20

I awoke to a persistent buzzing coming from next to my pillow. "Fuck, Vivian! Is that Peter again?"

"Sorry, I thought I turned my ringer off, I must have left it on vibrate," she moaned, muting her phone.

Just then, there was a knock at the door. "I don't even know why I try, I will never sleep again," I said to myself. I spent half the night drinking wine and waiting for Vivian to get home from her last shift working the local carnival. She now had another two weeks off before following the fair to its next location.

The knocking continued, and I yelled to my daughter. "Rosie, go get the door! I'm sure it's for you!" I heard the pitter patter of over-sized feet running down the hall, followed by the front door squeaking open.

"Mommy, can I go outside and play?" Rosie asked.

"Yes, but get dressed first, and tell your friend you only have an hour until I have to take you to your dad's house for the weekend," I said.

Rosie left her friend, Ivan, standing on our front porch leaning on his scooter. She scurried into her bedroom to throw on glittery leggings and a T-shirt dress.

Vivian pulled open the blinds to take a peek. "Oh, look at Ivan standing there by his new scooter, he thinks he's so cool. Rosie, Ivan thinks he is better than you!" she announced, loud enough for the boy to hear.

"He does?" Rosie asked.

"Yup! Look at his shiny new scooter. He's here to show it off because his is better than yours. You will never own one that cool!"

"Vivian, knock it off," I warned.

"No matter what you own, Rosie, Ivan's will always be better. His parents are rich and they can afford to buy him anything he wants."

I'm not sure where Vivian was coming up with her bullshit. Ivan lived in the same apartment complex as we did and wore cheap kid's clothes from Target like Rosie. I think she would have said anything to get a rise out of somebody. She wandered back into the bedroom and sat down next to me. "I hate that dumb kid. There is something wrong with him. Whenever I ask him a question, he ignores me."

Even though Vivian's breath wasn't particularly pleasant on a good day, today it smelled like her mouth hosted New York City's entire public sewer system.

I inched back. "Maybe it's because you intimidate him? He's been nothing but polite to me, he's shy."

"He's a little prick!" Vivian said. Rosie shut the front door as she left.

"Should I wear your extra swimsuit today?" Vivian asked. The water park season was coming to a close, and she had convinced me weeks ago to join her at Trickling Ponds on its last day. Despite my better judgment, I agreed. Since Rosie didn't want to go, we arranged it on a day she would be at her dad's house. I was jealous. Preparing for the worst, I stocked up on plenty of adult beverages to bring along with us.

"You should wear whatever makes you feel comfortable," I said. I prayed that she would just wear her men's style trunks and rash guard to avoid the negative attention she drew.

"I just don't know if I can pull off a woman's bathing suit yet," she admitted.

Not to be a dick about it, but without some serious reconstructive surgeries, waist training and voice lessons there was just no way Vivian would ever pull off being female. Believe me, I tried my damnedest to help her. I loved her to death, but she was living in a fantasy land.

That must have not been my lucky day because Vivian wore my extra suit. We were twins! If by twin I meant giant, broad shouldered, muscular-legged, long-footed, square-jawed man-lady with boobs. Well, at least we had the tits part in common.

"Do you mind driving?" Vivian asked, "I'm low on gas."

"I wanted to drink today."

"That's fine, baby girl, I'll drive your car back for you." That I could live with, so I agreed.

Once packed, I hustled Rosie into the car. After dropping her off for the weekend, I drove us the hour and a half to the water park. It was another blisteringly hot day and I couldn't wait to get my drink made and submerge my fat ass into the water. I had consumed more malt beverages than usual lately, and seeing myself in a bathing suit had been a sobering sight. It worried me that Vivian might look better in it than I did. Just kidding!

Trickling Ponds was at capacity, and all the parking spots in the main structure were filled. A park employee directed us to a small side lot a mile and a half from where we were headed. "Take the tram in," he said. The water park was on top of a hill, in an area that bordered a cattle farm. We had to navigate a narrow winding dirt road to the hidden parking lot. To make matters worse, I was now facing a bigger problem. Trickling Ponds checked bags upon entry and they did not allow you to bring in drinks. How was I going to smuggle in my tequila?

"You will have to drink it now, babe," Vivian decided.

"No way! I would die. Here," I said handing her the bottle. "Put it in the bottom of your backpack, under the towel.

"That won't work. They'll make me empty the bag." Vivian scoped out my body. "I'll stick it in the back of your suit!"

Although that sounded like a terrible idea at first, I must admit, that bitch was a genius! My bathing suit was tight due to my excess weight, and I had on a loosely fitting cover up that disguised the bottle perfectly.

We loaded onto the tram and were happy to find two empty rows together, one facing the other. It was like we had our own little train car. Our joy soon ended as a family of four boarded next to us. They took up the entirety of the bench seat directly across from where we were sitting. I noticed Vivian was becoming increasingly annoyed. She leaned her leg out and placed her feet on the bench across from us, taking over half their sitting space. They were polite and pretended like they didn't notice, huddling together and avoiding eye contact.

"Vivian, put your feet down, that's so rude!" I whispered in her ear. She kept them exactly where they were and acted like she couldn't hear me. Her smug smile gave it away. This made the tram ride uncomfortable for everyone involved except Vivian. Exiting couldn't come soon enough.

Once we successfully smuggled my tequila into Trickling Ponds, Vivian found a locker to rent. While she was setting the code, I spotted a frozen lemonade stand and eagerly took my wallet to make a purchase. Disappointment set in when I realized it was closed. Someone filled the booth floor to ceiling with dusty old boxes. Vivian joined me just seconds after I made the discovery. "What kind of shit hole is this?" she asked. "Why have lemonade stands if you aren't gonna sell lemonade?"

I giggled. "Well shit, what should I buy as a mixer?"

Vivian pointed out a self serving slushy stand. That was good enough for me! We entered the line. I looked around the tiny water park. "This place is old, huh?" I asked my girlfriend.

"I think they built it in the 1980s. They have not kept it up."

"No kidding, it's kind of scary!" Peering onto the ground, I added, "It looks like it needs to be re-cemented, see all the cracks?"

"Wait until we get into the wave pool, it will slice open our feet! Last time I came here, I limped for a week."

"I think I can do without the wave pool," I decided.

Finally, it was my turn to help myself to some slushy. I looked around but couldn't find a disposable cup anywhere. I walked over to the attendant, "Excuse me, where are the slushy cups?"

"We just have the twisty souvenir cups for $20."

I glanced at the overpriced, undersized, skinny pieces of hollow plastic. I couldn't make a drink in one of those. They were too tiny and expensive.

"No thanks. I would just like a regular cup please," I said.

"Okay. Go to the lunch area and order the cup. Once you get it, bring it back here to fill."

There was a giant line. "We can go straight to the front; we don't have to wait in another line, right?" Vivian asked the clerk.

"No. Wait in line again."

"We just waited for twenty minutes for nothing! Why would you have a slushy machine without cups? That is the dumbest thing I have ever heard of! Where is your manager?" she shouted. Several groups of park goers turned around to witness the commotion. I wanted to dig a hole in the ground and insert my head. The slushy attendant pointed us in the manager's direction. Vivian's attitude didn't change, and the manager refused to help us.

"I just want to get on an attraction, Asterisk! I hate that you are making us waste our time to feed your addiction."

"Why don't you go on a slide and I'll meet you at the exit afterwards," I suggested.

"No way! I have been on all the single rider slides before. I brought you here so I could go on the doubles. Vivian's eyes lit up. Go rent us a double tube, then we don't have to wait in line. Do it while I buy your cup!"

I left Vivian at the food stand and made my way to the rental booth. They had sold out for the day and I knew Vivian wouldn't take the news lightly. "This is the worst water park I have ever been to! I'm never coming here again. What a waste of money my season pass was."

I decided that I would just take whatever drink the stand was selling and forfeit the slushy just to move forward. I ended up with warm peach tea in a cup with a smashed top, incapable of supporting a lid. Once back to the locker, I mixed my pathetic cocktail. Upon inspection I noticed black specks and a piece of plastic in the bottom. I guessed they probably had taken this one out of the trash to teach Vivian a lesson. Here I was being the one to bear the bitch's burden. I picked the junk out of the cup and prayed the alcohol would kill whatever germs were inside.

"Have you ever been on a hydro-magnetic water slide before?" Vivian asked. She had the enthusiasm of a hawk making its first kill.

"No, I haven't."

"Let's go, girl!"

Whatever.

I followed Vivian to the slowest moving line I had ever been subjected to. Though it was only about fifty people deep, we stood for close to two hours. I noticed that everyone, but us, was under the age of eighteen. I was feeling old, awkward and out of place. Luckily, the younger generation didn't seem to think a transgender girl was weird. Vivian talked non-stop in a voice much louder than normal and every third word was a profanity. Although I did my best to remind her we were around children, it didn't have much of an impression.

I tried to down my crappy cocktail, but it was disgusting and hard to swallow. It was making me nauseous, so when Vivian swept it out of my hands and took a giant chug, I was almost grateful. Eventually we made it to the front of the line and entered the ride for the most unfulfilling twenty seconds in history.

"We waited two hours for that?" I asked.

"Right? So much for the hydro-magnetism! It's a total scam. What should we go on next?" Vivian grabbed my hand and led me off of the ride. "Oh! I know!"

"Wait, wait, wait," I begged. "I need a bathroom break, a new soda and a half hour to relax in the lazy river, please."

"Stop trying to ruin the day with your laziness!"

"I'm old!" I reminded her. "I'm not a spring chicken like you. I want to relax."

"Pfft, please, you are only three years older than me."

"But I'm a parent!" There was no other way out, I had to use my one "free pass" on Vivian. That's right! I asked her if she wanted to smoke a doobie. The next thing I knew we were on the long tram ride to the car. It was virtually empty. This time I put my feet up.

"I can't wait to get high!" Vivian admitted, "I bet it will be so much more fun here after we smoke a joint!"

A voice echoed from behind. "It's fun to be high! I used to love to get high. Can't get high no more though."

We turned around to see what appeared to be the female version of Crocodile Dundee, only with a case of schizophrenia. She had on a giant gray hat, over-sized sunglasses and a tan outfit made purely of khaki.

"Do you work for the park?" Vivian asked.

"Yup, I ride on this tram all day long. I can't get high though," she chuckled. She was bizarre, yet probably the most entertaining thing we had encountered all day.

"Why can't you get high?" I asked. "Marijuana is legal now."

"Oh no, never marijuana! Cocaine, acid, ecstasy, Special K. Wee hoo!"

Vivian and I looked at each other and laughed. Our new friend was laughing too.

"This is our stop," Vivian told her as the tram slowed. "We'll be heading back soon. Maybe we will see you then?"

"Getting high is fun but then it hurts your brain. I was jumping off the roof into my swimming pool with my sister but I hit my head. Now my sister is dead!" she laughed. Because of her thick pair of shades you couldn't really tell who she was talking to, if anybody. We hopped off the tram and headed to my car.

Soon it was time to re-board. We sat across from our new buddy. "How's it hanging?" I asked. It looked like she had never stopped talking. Actually, I'm sure she hadn't because she didn't acknowledge my question at all and instead continued her gibberish. "High as an angel in the sky. I'm floating when I'm high. My sister couldn't fly." Vivian and I were just the perfect amount of "high" to enjoy it.

Even though I was reluctant, I accompanied Vivian to the next ride. It was at least an hour before we reached the front of the line.

"Step on here, please." I looked over to where the ride attendant was pointing. Was he fucking serious? I glanced at Vivian for some kind of reaction, but she was following orders for once. Adjacent to the entrance of the ride was a giant scale. These jerks would weigh us before allowing us to ride.

"Sorry! You are too heavy!" he informed us, after reading our combined weight. That had to be the most horrific thing that had ever happened in my life. "What?" I asked. "You are too big to ride together. Exit the ride, please move along. Next!"

"Wait, wait!" I screamed. Now it was my turn to go psycho, "What is the weight limit for two people?"

"400 lbs. Please move, you are holding up the line!"

I glanced over to Vivian and looked her up and down. Exactly how much of the 400 was her fault? Worse yet, how much was mine?

"No! I will not moooove!" Like a mad birthing cow, I continued my intoxicated tirade. "We waited in line for an hour to ride this! There was not a weight limit posted anywhere in the line! None of the other employees working here bothered to pull me aside and tell me I was TOO FAT to get on! I'm not leaving until I get on a ride, any ride!"

Vivian's face was gleaming, my craziness had impressed her.

My tantrum also influenced the park employees. We were promptly escorted to the front of another water slide and the two of us climbed onto a giant inner tube together. "Remove your sunglasses!" A lifeguard said.

Just as I was pulling them off, they propelled us down the giant slide and an enormous force ripped my favorite pair of gold-rimmed shades right out of my hand. Before I could react to what had happened, we were already at the bottom of the ride floating in a foggy pool of over-chlorinated water. I jumped off the raft and violently searched through the waves.

"You must exit!" the lifeguard called out.

"I lost my sunglasses, I need to find them!"

"You can go to the lost and found after the park closes."

"Grrr! Can we please leave, now?" I begged Vivian.

Even though she hated the water park too, she was insistent on staying to get her money's worth. "Asterisk, I'm not coming back again because this place sucks too much. I have to at least stay a full day so I know the money spent on my season pass wasn't a complete waste!"

"So in essence, you are paying to torture yourself?" Finally, something I said made sense to her, and she agreed to leave. Unfortunately, we didn't see our new friend on the final tram ride back to the car. I never found my sunglasses either.

CHAPTER 21

The carnival had moved up north and, true to her word, Vivian had gone with them. Business died down, and she was barely getting enough hours to cover her car payments. Because of this, she moved back in right away. Though I worried about her financially, I was happy to have her home most nights. As the summer passed, I watched her go to countless interviews dressed as 'her' only to be rejected. Doing what I could to help, I scouted for trans-friendly jobs online and even reached out to various friends of mine who owned businesses and asked them to consider hiring her. Still, she wasn't having any luck. I felt terrible, and it caused me to worry what Rosie's future would be like. I was still paying the rent and utilities on my own, and I found that Vivian needed a few bucks "here and there" more and more often.

Vivian, being Vivian, didn't seem to let it get her down one bit, and even talked me into purchasing season passes to Happy Hills. They were only about $10 a month each, so I figured, "what the hell?" Vivian was ready to use them the following day. Rosie had to go to school, and wasn't interested in the theme park, anyway. She still feared roller coasters, so we left her behind.

"Rosie, the park closes at 6:00 pm, we won't be home until about 7:30. Will you be all right that late?"

"Yes, I'm not scared."

"Okay, I know this is the furthest I have ever gone when you have been home alone. Do you have your emergency contact numbers?"

"Yes."

"What are the rules?"

"Do my homework, lock the door, no friends inside and I don't go out, text you when I get out of school... Um, make a snack. I can use the microwave but not the oven?"

"Yes, and you can take your bath after we get back. I ordered you a pizza for dinner and paid for it. They will deliver it at 5:30, okay?"

"Yay! Thank you, Mommy!"

I sent my munchkin off to the bus stop and then packed my usual mini ice chest with tequila. I was thrilled to spend a day alone with my Barbie-clad, Ken-sized doll! I got mushy just thinking about her. I dug through my wardrobe and plucked out a brand new dress that fit my curves perfectly and a matching pair of rhinestone platforms. Once dressed, I gave my chick a big hug. She was busy digging through her own closet.

"Catch!" She threw me a thin orange blanket.

"Okay?" The skin on my fingers snagged against the cheap fabric.

"That's Ducks, baby! It's almost hockey season! I'll let you use that to keep warm at the stadium." I watched as she pulled out a jersey of the same colors, "You don't know this yet, but wearing a jersey to a game is the shit! It makes you the coolest person there!"

I blinked twice. I wasn't sure if I had transported back to high school. Nope, I was still in my thirties. "Is that what you are wearing today?" I asked her, only half-joking.

126

She ignored me. "I'm ready to go!" she said. "Can we take your car? I've put too many miles on mine this week." I knew that she meant she was out of gas again. "No problem, but you drive back!" I said, holding up my little ice chest with the tequila bottle sticking out.

Ninety minutes later we parked in the lot of Happy Hills and I reached for our cups. I was smarter by then and packed my own mixer. Once I dumped in the entire bottle of tequila and topped it with the zero-calorie margarita mix, I was ready to enter. I threw my wallet and keys into Vivian's backpack. I carried the drinks inside and attempted to hand Vivian hers when she stopped me.

"Oh no, thanks. I'm not drinking. I have a job interview tomorrow."

Her admission caught me by surprise, but I didn't care. "Well, I guess I'm getting drunk!"

And get drunk I did, but a bit too fast. I finished the first cup after only two rides, and on an empty stomach. I got a little giddy which annoyed Vivian. As I was talking to fellow coaster passengers, Vivian was feeling left out. Generally when we visited Happy Hills, we were on the same level, but since today she remained sober, she wasn't playing along.

"Let's get something to eat, Asterisk."

"I don't want food! I want beer!"

"After we eat I'll take you! " she said. "You are being a pain in the ass today. It's so annoying!"

We ordered our free meals from our season passes. I nibbled on mine but was more interested in intensifying my afternoon buzz. Once we made it to the bar, we each ordered. The bartender looked under twenty-one and had probably never poured before. He was holding two frosty mugs a good foot away from the taps while letting the beer drizzle into the glasses; they were all foam.

"Vivian! Vivian! Look at that kid trying to pour! Oh, my God! Don't they train them here? He's ruining it! He's wasting the keg! We need to tell him, Vivian! Vivian!"

"Shut the fuck up, Asterisk! He's pouring the beer just fine! Finish up so we can go on another ride!"

"No, he's not. Oh, I can't watch this! Tilt the glass! Tilt the glass!"

"Dude, I said I want to go on some coasters!" Vivian repeated.

"I want to go somewhere else," I said. "I'm bored with the rides. Can we hit up a brewery or a bar or... any grown up place?"

"You are a fucking drunk, Asterisk! You are wrecking my day you stupid bitch."

"Fuck you, Vivian!" I grabbed my keys out of her bag and took off, headed towards the exit. I hiked the long hill to the parking lot, climbed into the passenger seat of my SUV and passed out.

The next thing I remember is sitting in the back of a police car wearing handcuffs. "Vivian!" I screamed, "Vivian, where are you?" In front of me I could see my car doors were open and on top of my SUV was the tiny cooler, the empty bottle of tequila and Vivian's bong. Red and blue lights were flashing all around. A few minutes later a police officer entered the front seat of the patrol car.

"Where is Vivian?" I asked.

"I'd like to know the same thing!" he said, with a chuckle. "Who is this mysterious Vivian, and where did she run off to?"

"She was driving, she was my designated driver!"

"Oh, I don't think she was behind the wheel."

I watched him pick up the microphone to his police radio, "Yeah her car is banged up, but she's okay."

Who was he talking about? "Am I going to jail? I have to be to work tomorrow."

"You won't make it to work, honey."

"Vivian was driving!" I tried again.

"You keep talking about this Vivian but I haven't seen her."

"She's my girlfriend, she's transgender..."

Glancing around, I realized it was nighttime, but I was awake. In my last memory it was still early afternoon. The officer laughed again, shaking his head. "I'm doing you a favor," he said, while lifting my cell phone to show me. I could see it was on his charger. "Your phone was dead, I will charge it on the way to the station and then I'll turn it off. That way you can call someone in the morning."

It rang. "What do you know? It's the mysterious 'Vivian'."

"Answer it!"

"You'll have to wait until you're booked to make a call. I can't believe this is a real person. Wow."

"She can tell you she was driving!"

I sat in the holding cell at the jail for hours. All I could think about was Rosie, and how scared she was. I still didn't know what happened or why I was in jail. If Vivian wasn't with me, she must be with Rosie, right?

"Five! Ms. Five!" a guard called out. I walked toward the little window in the far end of the room.

"I have your cell phone here. Let me know who you want to call and you can pull out the number," he was pointing to an old pay phone hanging on the wall.

"Can I have two numbers please?" The guard was accommodating.

First, I tried Rosie's cell, but there was no answer. Figuring that it must have been after her bedtime by now, I called Vivian.

"Hello?" she sounded hysterical.

"Vivian! What happened to me? Where did you go? I thought you were my driver!"

"You punched me, Asterisk."

"I did what?"

"You punched me in my face, so I left."

"Where's Rosie? Are you at home?"

"I left Rosie alone at the apartment. I'm sorry to tell you this right now but I moved my stuff out. I left you. It's over, Asterisk. I want you to know that this hurts me too!"

I took a deep breath. "Is Rosie okay?"

"I left her at home asleep."

"What time is it?" I asked.

"It's 3:00 in the morning, Asterisk."

"Oh, my God! You can't leave Rosie alone like that! It will scare her to death. Go back there! Please go spend the night with her and get her to school in the morning!" Vivian was crying, "I will do that! I will do that for you!"

"They are charging me with driving under the influence. The guard said they will release me in the morning. Can you come get me? I lost my shoes and I don't know where my car is!"

"I have a job interview," she reminded me. "You are sixty miles away. Figure it out yourself."

"But I don't have shoes or any money!" My eyes were welling up.

"Call me when you get out, I'll see what I can do but I'm broke, and almost out of gas," she finally admitted.

I hung up the phone, and the guard approached the door. "Let's go." He handed me a dirty green blanket. The material resembled the hockey one Vivian had shown me earlier. I was led to a tiny cell. It was cold, bright and filthy. I rolled myself into a ball on the only vacant bed. "Please try to sleep through this," I begged myself, but it was no use. I had missed two doses of my medication and I thought my heart might explode at any second. My pulse was racing so fast that my entire body trembled.

Not long after I entered the room, the woman on the bunk above mine climbed down, crawled to the filthy shared toilet inside our cell and vomited. The smell hit me instantly and my stomach churned. After five minutes had passed, she crawled away and climbed back into her bed above mine. The entire frame convulsed with her body. She was moaning and rocking back and forth in agony. It didn't take long for her to climb down and resume her spot in front of the toilet. I was astounded by how much sick could come from such a small person.

My mouth was dry, and I needed water. The upper part of the toilet was a drinking fountain. My bladder was full, and I needed release, but there was no way I would ask her to move. The vomiting seemed like it would never end, and it didn't. I could hear her calling out to the guards for help. "I need my blood pressure meds!" she howled in between fits of sickness, but no one responded. I prayed that I wouldn't have a heart attack because I realized if I did, no one would come to my aid. The entire night, all I could think of was Rosie alone and what a failure I was as a mom.

Seven hours later, they removed me from the cell. "Five, Asterisk Five! We heard about you!" The releasing officer smirked. He took me into a small room and began the discharge process. After handing me a plastic bag containing my belongings, he directed me to change back into my own clothes. I exited a few minutes later and resumed my seat on the bench.

"Where are your shoes?" he asked.

"I don't know."

"Call someone and have them bring you a pair."

"I don't think anyone will come for me, I live over an hour from here."

He let out a sigh, "Okay, where is your car?"

"I'm not sure."

"Let's see what I can find out." The policeman returned a few minutes later with a piece of paper containing an address. They left my car sitting in the parking lot of where I was arrested. The officer hadn't towed it, but that didn't mean the landlord hadn't later in the night.

I didn't have shoes, and the location was six miles away, I couldn't walk. My phone had just enough charge to order an Uber. Not sure any driver would be willing to pick someone up in front of the jail, I kept my fingers crossed and paced barefoot back and forth in front of the window. When the car pulled up, I thanked my lucky stars.

"Wow, what happened?" the operator asked as I entered the vehicle.

"Rough night," I admitted. "Thanks for picking me up."

"What happened?" he asked.

Feeling ashamed and knowing I wouldn't see him again, I thought, "What the hell?" and purged my sin. "They arrested me for driving under the influence last night."

"Oh, wow! You didn't have a designated driver?" he asked.

"I did, but we got into a fight and they left me alone."

"Don't tell me this was some dirt bag guy, was it?"

"Uh, yeah...?" I wasn't sure how to answer.

"Listen honey," the driver began, "a beautiful girl like you doesn't need some scum bag guy who treats her like shit and can't take care of her after she's had a few. You can do better than that. Find someone who treats you the way you deserve."

"Beautiful?" Why I had just seen my mug shot, and it was a sobering sight. I had black makeup smudged under my eyes, my hair was a mess and my dress wrinkled. I resembled an evil crack-smoking clown.

"Jesus knows that we make mistakes, that's why he died on the cross for our sins."

I was now regretting the purge.

"But you can't let your mistakes keep you down! Jesus wants you to lift yourself back up!"

He had a point.

"Here we are, what does your car look like?" he asked, pulling into the lot.

"It's right there!" A huge cloud lifted off my shoulders upon seeing my SUV.

"Where is the damage at?" he asked.

"I think they said I hit something, but I don't remember what. So it must be in the front."

He ventured out with me and walked around my car. Once we saw the bumper, it was obvious where it had hit. Though it was still roadworthy, it had been my first new car, and not yet a year old. The shame engulfed me. "Can you tell me how to get to the freeway from here?" I asked. "My phone is dead."

"Yup! Just over this hill and make a left. Good luck to you, and God bless!"

I climbed into the car and put my cell phone on the charger. The engine started, and I was grateful it ran. I followed his directions and made it onto the freeway. After the phone had a charge I called Vivian. "You out?" she asked.

"Yes, how did the interview go?"

"I nailed it! I'm sure they will hire me."

"That's great. Congratulations. I'm almost at the apartment. Where are you now?"

"I was thinking about heading back there."

"Can we talk? Please?" There was a long pause. "Please, Vivian. I promise I will quit drinking. Yesterday was my last one. I'm done."

"All right girl, we can talk. If you want to quit, I will help you. I'll meet you back at the apartment in a few."

CHAPTER 22

W hen I stepped through the door to my apartment, Vivian was already there. I gave her a big hug. She held me for a second before forcing me away. "Ew! You stink like a prison, go shower and change your clothes before you touch me again."

"I know, I'm sorry," I apologized, while pulling off my dress. I walked into the bathroom to run the water. "I'm starving," I said to Vivian, before turning on the faucet.

"Didn't care much for the bologna sandwich, huh? Well, hurry and we can get lunch."

"I don't want to leave the apartment. Can we order in?" I asked.

"Where's your debit card?"

"It's in my bag."

By the time I was out of the shower, Vivian had called in the order.

"Can I have a hug now?"

"I guess," she said, placing her long arms around me. "Ow!" she screamed after I kissed her face.

"What?"

"That's where you hit me!"

I pushed her long hair to take a peek at her injury, but I couldn't find any marks. "I'm so sorry, baby. I don't remember hitting you. Why did I do it?" I asked.

"I don't know! You were being ugly and making fun of me to strangers. You made me cry! It was so embarrassing, you wouldn't go on any rides. You just kept screaming, 'Bar! Bar! I want to go to the bar!' over and over again!"

"I'm so sorry."

"I won't stay in an abusive relationship, Asterisk! If you will actually stop drinking and promise never to be violent towards me again, I'll stay."

"I promise."

"Okay. Can you help me move my things back in?"

As I hung up her T-shirts, I searched for more answers. "I don't remember much more than being at the bar, having a beer with you."

"That's the last thing you remember? Wow. Well, you were crazy, yelling at people. Do you remember screaming at the poor bartender? You kept telling him he didn't know how to pour drinks. Then you disappeared. After a while I started to look for you. I found you in the car, passed out. I couldn't believe it. I woke you up to go on more rides."

"Why didn't you let me sleep?" I asked.

"It was still early in the day! You needed to eat something to soak up the alcohol. Anyway, after I woke you up, you acted nuts, yelling at me, calling me a sociopath. You were running around all crazy!"

"Then why didn't you bring me home?"

"How was I supposed to do that when you wouldn't listen to me?"

"Um... Maybe throw me in the back seat and lock the door?"

"I'm not a man!" she shouted. "It's not my job to corral you. Anyway, I was sober the whole time! You insisted on driving, but you were swerving around the parking lot and almost hit people, do you remember that?"

"You were sober and you let me drive?" None of this computed.

"You wouldn't let me! I was trying to get you to go to my favorite restaurant. You needed to eat but instead, you pulled up to a McDonald's. We walked inside together. I asked you why we were there and you shouted at me, saying I had been the one that wanted to go there! I told you again, there was a great place I wanted to go to, but you weren't making any sense! Then you hit me so I told you I was leaving. You drove away, and I called my friend to give me a ride back to the apartment. If I had been the one to hit you, you would have done the same!" she defended herself.

"No, Vivian! If you were drunk, I wouldn't have left you! You deserted me. I feel devastated by your betrayal. When you love someone you care for them, you make sure they are okay."

"I don't understand."

That was probably the only honest statement she ever made.

"I know you don't, you can't. Your brain just doesn't work like," I wanted to say: "a normal person's," but caught myself. "Your brain doesn't work like mine, it's different."

Just then Rosie walked through the door. My eyes lit up. "Rosie, I'm so sorry!"

"Yay! Mommy is back! It's okay. Vivian said you were in jail."

"Damn right! I'm not here to sugarcoat anything. Your mom needs to own up to what she did! Do you remember me waking you up last night, Rosie?"

"No."

"You don't?" Vivian asked, feigning shock. "I woke you up before I left and told you your mom is an alcoholic and that I couldn't help her but you needed to! You had to be strong and tell her she needs to quit drinking!"

Rosie glanced my way with a helpless look across her face. "Vivian only left for a few minutes honey, she was angry at me. But she came back. You didn't sleep here alone," I tried consoling her. "I messed up, I made a tremendous mistake and I'm very sorry. It won't happen again. I'm not drinking anymore."

"Why were you in jail?" she asked.

"Because I drank alcohol and drove my car."

Rosie was even more confused, "But Vivian always drives."

"Your mom punched me!" Vivian yelled. "She hit me in the face!"

"Good," Rosie stated.

In the days that followed, tensions between Rosie and Vivian escalated. Things had never been the same since Rosie walked in on Vivian and I having sex but now that Vivian had crossed the line with me, Rosie was on the attack.

I was at work a few days later when I received a text from my daughter. "Mommy, Vivian is being rude and she's trying to tell me what to do again."

"Okay, I'll talk to her," I promised.

"Thank you, Mommy."

That night I told Vivian in the nicest way imaginable, that if she needed Rosie to do something around the house, to inform me and I would tell Rosie myself.

"Ew, Mommy! Vivian just went to the bathroom and didn't wash her hands!"

"Vivian is an adult honey, you can't tell her what to do!" I leaned into

Vivian and whispered, "Please wash your hands, you are setting a bad example."

Our sex life had changed drastically too. We were making out on my couch a few nights later, when I leaned into her to get more comfortable.

"Ah! Get off me! You are pulling my hair!" she shrieked. I stood up and headed towards the kitchen to pour myself some water.

"Where did you go? What are you doing?" she asked, in her 'lady' voice.

"You freaked me out," I said. "I'm not in the mood anymore."

"Come here." She whined, "Rape me! Rape me!"

I stared back at her on my bed with her crooked face and double chin, her strange breasts exposed atop of her masculine chest and suddenly she seemed grotesque. Like a man would, she reached out and forced me against her. She attempted to kiss me but it felt more like a dog slobbering down my neck. I could smell that New York sewer rot drifting from her mouth and onto my body. I suddenly wanted to puke.

"Come on!" she begged, "I want to put my 'clit' in you."

I gave in and let her try, just to stop her from drooling on me. Once she was on top, it was a challenge for her to keep herself hard enough to penetrate me. As I usually did, I grabbed her by the ass and forced her hips inside my own.

"Ow! Stop it!" she screamed. "Your leg is hurting me!"

"I'm fucking the devil," I thought to myself.

Close to a week had gone by since my arrest. My sobriety had settled in and everything around me became a little more clear. I no longer saw Vivian as a fun and exciting addition to my life. Instead, she was a parasite sucking the life out of Rosie and me. The more I gave her the more she wanted, yet she had nothing to give us in return.

I was getting ready to leave work when a text came in from Rosie. It was a picture of my unmade bed. The caption read, "How come I have to do chores all the time, and Vivian doesn't even have to make the bed?"

I thought it was hilarious and sent a screenshot to Vivian. "Rosie sent me this, 'BUSTED!'" I wrote along with it.

"What the fuck? Why are you always teaming up against me?" Vivian replied.

"Oh honey, I wasn't trying to hurt you, I figured you would laugh. It's not a big deal."

"It is a big deal! I can't do anything right!"

Vivian sounded like a five-year-old. I felt like the parent of two tween-aged transgender daughters. I picked up the phone and called her. "What?" she answered, with the matching attitude.

"Don't be angry, I love you!"

"Whatever. Hey listen, I drove to the liquor store today to cash in the $10 lottery ticket you left on the table and it wasn't a winner." I knew she was lying.

"Yes, it is. I'll look at it myself when I get home."

"I threw it away."

There it was.

"It was a loser, Asterisk. I even scratched off the bar code and had the clerk at the store scan it into the machine to make sure."

I could remember scratching the bar code myself. I always did that on the winning tickets."Vivian, why are you lying? I already told you, you could keep the money. It's not a big deal. Don't I always give you everything you ask for?"

"If you think I'm a liar, why even have me around?"

"Because I love you and love is unconditional." I changed the subject. "Can you turn off the crock pot and boil some water for noodles? When I get home, I want to mix some sour cream into the sauce after it cools down."

"You can boil them when you get back."

"Okay, but it will take longer for us to eat."

Vivian let out a sigh, "Fine. I'll do it."

I arrived home thirty minutes later. Vivian had already cooked the noodles. She tried handing me a big bowl with the half-made sauce on top. "Oh, shit Vivian! Stop! The sauce isn't finished!" I noticed Rosie sitting at the table nibbling on a giant bowl of her own. She scrunched her nose. "This food tastes weird!"

"Yeah, because I didn't finish adding the cream! Vivian please stop, you are spoiling it!"

Vivian slammed the bowl down, stormed into my room and threw herself onto my bed. I followed her. "Please don't do this, let's just have dinner. I want to have a nice night."

Vivian crossed her arms over her chest. "I made you dinner, and you went off on me for no reason!"

That was it; the final straw. All the anger I had been bottling up inside our entire relationship was about to release itself.

"YOU MADE ME DINNER? YOU? I HAD THE FUCKING SAUCE COOKING IN THAT CROCK POT FOR TEN HOURS! ALL YOU HAD TO DO WAS BOIL THE NOODLES AND YOU FUCKED IT UP ON PURPOSE! THAT'S IT VIVIAN! PACK YOUR SHIT RIGHT NOW AND GET OUT OF MY HOME!"

"I'm sorry," she rolled her eyes.

I just shook my head, "Get out!"

I sent Rosie to her room and watched Vivian pack up her things. When she finished, she asked me, "Can I leave my TV here? It won't fit in my car. I can get it tomorrow?"

"Nope! I'd like my key back please." She handed me her key ring, and I removed it myself.

As she was walking out the door for the final time, she leaned in to hug me. This time I hugged her back.

"You don't love me Vivian. You never have and you never will, your brain is broke."

"You don't believe anybody loves you."

"Rosie loves me! My cat loves me!"

"...and someone else loves you too." I'm still not sure if she was trying to reference herself, but at that moment something bizarre happened. I looked into her usually vivid blue eyes and they were dead cold. Empty. I'll never forget, it was haunting.

Suddenly, 'she' had disappeared and the surfer dude was back. He bobbed his head in a way that made his long hair sway. His eyes resembled those of a corpse as he talked. "Always remember you are beautiful. Let no one tell you different! You are great the way you are. I'll always be your friend. Stay positive girl. See you around!"

And just like that, Vivian was out of our lives.

CHAPTER 23

Even though I'd been fed up with Vivian, I hated that she was gone. Everything was so desolate and silent without her around. I did my best to move forward by working out in the evenings and writing. Still, I couldn't force her out of my brain. I needed to see her face. I logged onto Instagram only to discover she had blocked me. What a bitch! I Googled her name and her public feed came up. My heart sank when I saw it, "Single trans lesbian, seeking girlfriend." It had only been days since she left and already she was searching for someone new. As I had been grieving and distressed, she was on the prowl for someone else to use. I don't know why it stunned me so much, I knew she was messed up from the get-go.

While out for my night jog, a song played through my headphones that reminded me of her. I broke down and sent her a text. "You are a horrible person, Vivian! Already looking for someone new? I'm canceling your car insurance. Consider this your five days' notice. I'll have my agent call you, and you can get your own policy."

"You broke up with me, remember? I didn't do anything to you. You just went nuts. Whatever, I can't afford insurance. Do what you want."

"I didn't 'go nuts!' It was a heightened response from months of receiving your abuse!"

"Ugh, remember you are the abuser, Asterisk, you are the one who punched me. I won't waste my energy arguing with you. It's over. Bye."

"Return my concert ticket, I want to go to Rising Fly. It's a huge venue, we won't run into each other."

Vivian didn't reply, she had already blocked my number.

The next week, I took Rosie to visit the endocrinologist.

"Hi Rosie. I'm Dr. Chadwick," he introduced himself, displaying a dopey grin. I noticed white crusty stuff caked in the edges of his mouth. Some of it flew our way as he spoke.

"It looks like you fit the criteria of being a transgender person, and hormone therapy seems to be the universal way to proceed," he peered through her medical file. "I recommend it. Has anyone explained the treatment to you?"

Rosie nodded.

I spoke up. "Yes, we have been thoroughly informed. Rosie spent six months in therapy at the LGBTQ center, followed by more recent sessions with the therapist in your office. We have been to group meetings and attended events with informational speakers."

"That's wonderful!"

"Oh, and my ex girlfriend is transgender, so Rosie has experienced firsthand what female hormones do to the male body."

Dr. Chadwick pondered my words for a moment before he spoke, "Wow. That's unusual. I mean for someone to be related to, or even know one transgender person is so rare, but two. Wow. That's great." He continued, "So Rosie, you know that female hormones change the way your body will develop permanently? Instead of reaching puberty and maturing into a man, female hormones will help you develop differently. The fat deposits in your body will become more woman like and body hair growth will slow down in certain areas, like your face."

"And you won't be as tall!" I chimed in.

"That's not true, actually the hormones can't affect bone formation. Height is predetermined by DNA," the doctor explained.

"Aww crap, all the men on both sides of her family are over six feet tall!"

"Well, one element that can cause a stunt in a child's growth is obesity. Rosie, you are considered medically obese at your present weight," Dr. Chadwick said.

My face lit up. "You hear that? Being overweight will make you shorter!" I turned back to Rosie's physician, "Her entire life, doctors have lectured us for her being at the top of the growth charts, now we found out it's a good thing!"

"Wait, did I just say that? I guess I did." We both laughed.

"Hey Rosie," I said. "We can stop for some brownies on the way home!"

"Really?" She asked.

"The first thing we need to determine is if you are currently going through puberty. To perform sex reassignment surgery, there has to be a certain amount of growth 'down below' to have sufficient tissue to work with. We don't offer bottom surgery until a child is over eighteen and has been on female hormones for at least three years, however prior to female hormones we start a process called 'blockers'. A child can take hormone blockers for a long time. They are reversible because their only role is to put puberty 'on pause', if you will. They don't add or take away anything. Female hormones, however, are non-reversible."

Rosie and I nodded. We had already endured this lecture a million times.

"There are three ways to check to see if puberty has begun. One is by blood work, which you'll do in the lab."

Rosie looked horrified, "I hate needles!"

"Yeah me too, but you can just look away. Then all you feel is the prick. I'll distract you by making funny faces. They collect your blood in cool little vials," I said, trying to calm my kid.

Dr. Chadwick laughed again. "Your mom is funny, 'little vials'! It's not a torture chamber. We just take a few samples. The second test is a bone x-ray of the hand. It will allow us to figure out how far your body has already grown and how much more you will grow. It helps us to establish what your maximum height will be. We'll schedule them for next week. Today, I will perform a physical to find out if your testicles have dropped."

The doctor reached for a pair of disposable gloves and pulled them on. He picked up what appeared to be a necklace of various sized wooden balls. "What I need you to do Rosie, is pull up your dress, and remove your underwear so I can give the exam. I will lightly squeeze your testicles in my right hand and compare them to these balls with my left, as to determine your current size."

Rosie started to cry. They hadn't prepared us for this exam. "Come on, it's okay," I tried to soothe her.

Shaking, she slowly followed instruction. Once the doctor touched her 'private parts' she clamped her legs together. "Rosie, it's okay, I promise It'll be fast, just try to relax for ten seconds."

But it was of no use. Rosie couldn't loosen up, and who could blame her? Dr. Chadwick asked her to lie down, so he could try to test from a different angle. Once he finally got his hand around her gonads, he felt nothing. "Well, it's the first time I've come across this situation. Perhaps she hasn't dropped at all, or she might not have testicles."

"That could explain her body dysphoria!" I exclaimed.

"I guess we will go by the blood work. Most likely they just haven't descended yet and are being hidden somewhere within her fatty tissue. The nurse can set up the appointment on your way out."

After removing his gloves and washing his hands, he reached out to shake

Rosie's. "It was nice meeting you both!" She wasn't having any of it and instead turned away. I shook his hand, feeling guilt for having subjected my offspring to this necessary humiliation.

Once to the car, Rosie asked, "Where are we getting the brownies?" I chuckled. Later that evening, when she was calm, I sent Rosie in for a warm bath. After several minutes had passed, I tapped on the bathroom door.

"Yes, Mommy?"

"Rosie, while you are relaxed, try touching yourself where the doctor did. See if you can find your testicles."

"Okay, Mommy."

I had just regained my place on the couch when Rosie came bursting out of the bathroom in a towel. "I found them! I found my balls! I HAVE BALLS!"

That was probably the only time a trans girl had ever been excited about that.

CHAPTER 24

The days turned into weeks. I maintained my vigorous workout routine, binge-watched television shows and wrote like a madwoman. Within weeks I had melted off fifteen beer pounds. Every so often I would text message Vivian, asking how she was doing, but she never responded. My mind constantly drifted between devastation and hate. I secretly wished she would wreck her car and suffer the repercussions of not carrying the insurance. That would teach her.

I couldn't help myself and secretly Googled her online updates every day. Vivian was back living in her car but it didn't seem to phase her one bit. Along with her daily makeup clad selfies, she posted her most recent check-ins at all the local amusement parks, restaurants, hockey games and finally videos of the Rising Fly concert. That bitch had gone too far. I was lonely, depressed and bitter.

So on one particular day, three months after she had moved out, she posted a picture of her car's melted engine. She had towed it to a dealership several hours north of where I lived. First, I whooped like a drunken hyena after a kill. Then the guilt set in. I realized this was all my fault. I was the one who cut off the car insurance and wished her the worst. Damn it! I had to make things right. After a day of contemplating, I sent her an email.

"I hope you are okay. Let me know if you need help."

Minutes later she emailed me back. "Hey Five! I miss you, girl. You won't believe it, my car caught fire and practically blew up on the side of the freeway. The dealership thinks it's totaled. I'm stranded out here in the ghetto but otherwise fine. They are letting me drive a loaner, I've been sleeping in it. Stay positive girl!"

I pretended like I didn't already know.

"Oh, my God, how terrible! Do you need money?" Seconds later, my phone rang.

We chatted for hours and then, just like the start of our relationship, Vivian called me nightly. "When my car caught fire, I was on my way up north to move in with family. I just can't make it in California on my own, it's too expensive to live here. It's impossible! But I can't go to Oregon either, I'll be trapped at the house without a car. Nothing is in walking distance. My family still doesn't accept me as 'her'. I'll kill someone, or I'll kill myself."

"Everything will work out," I encouraged her. "Your car was only two years old. Cars just don't blow up. The company has to pay for it."

"I know, right? It was serviced at another dealership before I left town, they have the record of that!" Thinking back, in the six months I lived with Vivian, she never once took her car in for an oil change. I did some research and found there was a recall on Vivian's vehicle and sent the information her way. "I'm gonna make an insurance claim," she said. "I will tell them it wasn't canceled, it should have been reinstated. We had a 'lover's quarrel,' but made up. Just go along with it, okay?" she begged.

"No Vivian. I can't lie about that. I don't think it should be an insurance issue, your car is practically new."

"Please Asterisk, do this for me. I'll owe you big time! More than I already owe you now. Please, say you will!"

"Okay. I will," I lied.

Six days passed and still the dealership hadn't determined how to handle Vivian's car situation. One thing was for certain, it would never run again.

When the insurance company called to confirm Vivian's story, I had no choice but to tell the truth. I didn't want to go to prison for fraud, nor need my rates to rise because of her accident. It was going to be tripled due to the DUI insurance I now had to carry for the next three years.

"Did they call you?" Vivian asked.

"No, I'm sorry, they haven't." I lied.

"Okay, but when they do, you know what to tell them. We had a fight, and you added me back on."

Although she could be a complete shit, chatting with Vivian every day made me recognize how much I missed her. All the unhealthy parts of our relationship withered away, and it was as amazing as it was when we first met. She had me laughing constantly, and we built each other up with positive energy. So when she complained of monotony, being stuck out in the boonies, and having to spend the upcoming weekend alone, I asked her to visit.

"Really? You want me to come see you?"

"Yes, and I'll cover the gas, get down here you sexy bitch!"

"Okay. I'm leaving right now. I'll be there in eight hours."

After we hung up, I went into Rosie's room to talk about Vivian's arrival. "I guess it's okay if she comes for a little bit, but tell her she needs to be nice to me."

"She will be, or I'll throw her out!"

"Promise?"

"Yes."

Rosie was snoring when Vivian arrived. She greeted me with a giant hug and a long kiss. Within minutes we were naked in my bed together rubbing each other's nipples and making out. After Vivian slipped herself inside me, we came simultaneously and fell asleep holding hands.

Suddenly, we were jolted out of our slumber by the heavy thundering of Rosie's voice. "Eww! what's that smell? Vivian your breath STINKS! The whole house stinks!"

"It's nice to see you too, Rosie!" Vivian said.

"Rosie you are being vulgar," I scolded.

"Wait until you take female hormones, Rosie. We will see how you smell! Anyway, my breath is nothing compared to the stench from your ass! Go clog the toilet again."

"Both of you, enough! Holy shit! Rosie, get dressed and head to the bus stop. It leaves in fifteen minutes!" Rosie stuck her tongue out at Vivian and stomped off to get ready for school.

CHAPTER 25

We awoke to the loud buzzing of Vivian's phone. "Is that your dumb friend Peter again? I think he's in love with you."

"Asterisk! Shh!" Vivian demanded. "I think it's the dealership calling about the car." My muscular mama jumped out of bed and ran into the bathroom for privacy. She was wearing nothing but a black lace thong. The bitch had better underwear than I did, and a firmer butt.

Vivian's screams resonated from the small room. She followed them up with wailing cries. When she shouted; "Fucking Asshole!" I knew she hung up. Feeling lazy and not wanting to get out of bed, I sent her a text. "What happened?"

Instead of texting back, Vivian screamed, "I'll tell you in a minute, I'm going to the bathroom. Why the fuck would you message me from the bedroom?"

I checked my emails and giggled to myself as I waited. Vivian was still on the crapper when she began the loud phone conversation with her father. The toilet flushed and she opened the door, making her way back to my bed. She gave me a look that said, "I can't believe this shit," and set her phone to speaker mode. She placed her finger on her lips to "shush" me, while allowing me to listen. "Dad, they still won't fix my car! I have their loaner and they want it back as soon as possible. I need some money for another hotel room."

Her father's speech was slow and monotone with just a tinge of a southern inflection. "Son, I already sent you money last week. What you need is to move here and get your life together. You're too old for this mumbo jumbo."

"I'm not your son, I'm your daughter. My name is Vivian, remember?"

"Listen to me boy, you need to get your head on straight. No more of this talking nonsense. You have a whole family here in Oregon who wants to see you. All of us want to be in your life. Now, I told you, I will drive down myself to get you and tow your car back with us."

"Dad, I gotta go. My phone is broke and it won't hold a charge," she lied, simultaneously flipping her dad 'the bird' through the phone.

"Son listen to me, right as we speak I'm looking at a nice cellular I just replaced, there's nothing wrong with it, it's just as new as the one you have. This phone will be yours, once you get here."

"What dad? I can't understand you, you are breaking up." CLICK!

Even with her absence of maturity, I found myself once again feeling bad for my little prostate princess. "Holy shit! That's the way he treats you? You can't move there!"

"Where else can I go, Asterisk. The dealership wants the car back tomorrow morning."

"Take it! Then fly back here." I wasn't about to lose Vivian again.

"I can't afford to."

I let out a sigh, "I'll give you the money. Just come back home."

That afternoon, Vivian found a cheap one-way airline ticket for the following day. She left around midnight to do the eight-hour drive to the dealership. The next day, I picked her up from the airport on my lunch break.

"Aww Five, you missed me these past months, didn't you?"

"I know things didn't work out before, but this time we need each other."

It was true. Vivian was now without a car and I had my court date the following week. My driver's license was about to be revoked, and I needed a way to get to work. The carnival had ended and Vivian was without an income. We were both trapped.

"Will you go to court with me," I asked. "The judge will take my license away and I won't be able to drive home. The courts allow police officers to wait in the parking lot to see if you try to drive, if you do, they arrest you!"

"I've heard that, what do you expect? They are fucking pigs, it's a fascist state!"

I nodded, "I'm scared."

"It'll be fine, Asterisk. You didn't hit anyone, if you did they would've made a claim on your insurance by now. Yes, I'll go with you. The court house is down the street from Happy Hills! We can go after, ride coasters and get lunch."

"I don't think I'll be up for it after a day in court. It'll take up most of the afternoon, and the traffic home will be insane."

"Come on Asterisk, we can wait out traffic at the park. I'll let you get a beer."

"Really?" I asked.

"Yup! You haven't had a drink since the night you went to jail. I'm proud of you, I didn't think you could do it!"

I scrunched my eyebrows, "Why not?"

"I don't know. Because you drank every day?"

"Then why do you trust me to start again?"

"It's only one, and it will be with me. You can drink once in a while. Just don't go crazy."

"One won't work for me," I concluded. "I weigh too much, I'll need at least two to catch a buzz."

Vivian giggled, "Fine you can have two."

"How about three?" We both laughed.

I picked up my cell and dialed my insurance company. I added Vivian back onto my policy, this time for coverage on my own car.

CHAPTER 26

"**W**hat?" Vivian asked. She was half asleep and curled sideways on my bed. I waited while she pressed her leopard clad ass into the air and stretched.

"It's time to get ready. I have court today." I nudged her.

"Ew, stop pushing me. I'll get up," she moaned. After opening her eyes, she caught sight of my cat snoozing on the pillow next to hers. "Get the fuck off!" She yelled, sounding more like my dad than my girlfriend. After successfully swatting my animal away, she jumped up and headed into the bathroom to take a shower.

"Don't take two hours again," I warned. "We have to leave in forty minutes."

"Then you should have woken me up early."

My pulse had been racing for hours, keeping me awake most of the night. With my eyes crusted over, I met Vivian in the bathroom, opening the door and turning on the fan to let out the steam from the hot water. I wiped off the mirror and pulled out my box of makeup. Despite her morning tantrum, Vivian was ready on time. I dressed as conservatively as possible. Vivian didn't follow my lead, she was wearing a black studded blouse, leather skirt, and neon blue lipstick.

I grimaced while noting her wardrobe selection. "Don't worry, they won't care about what I'm wearing, I'm not the one appearing before the judge," she said. We loaded into my car and headed the sixty miles in heavy morning traffic. I tried to enjoy the drive realizing it would be my last time behind the wheel for the next several months. Once at the courthouse, my body trembled with anxiety. Vivian didn't seem to notice and spent her time scrolling through Instagram, until the deputy finally recommended she put her phone away. "How do I request a public defender?" I asked. He handed me a clipboard and advised me to add my name to the list while I waited.

After stowing her phone in her purse, she whispered about how bored she was. The stench from her mouth hit me like a wall. I anticipated a trail of green fog swarming around her with flies. It smelled like a rotting carcass after sitting out in the sun for five days. I reached into my bag, pulled out a box of mints, and handed one to her.

"No thanks. I don't like those."

Once again, I was nasally assaulted. "Please?" I begged. With a huff, she snatched the peppermint out of my hand and placed it in between her aqua lips.

Minutes turned into hours and the judge still hadn't called my name. It was nearing noon when the court warned they would take an hour recess for lunch. At the last second, they guided me into the hall by the public defender. "Let me read the charges to you quickly. A man called in what appeared to be a drunk driver. Found a woman standing outside of her vehicle. She was not cooperative. Police were called onto the scene. Woman appeared intoxicated and was subjected to field sobriety tests which she failed. Damage to the vehicle suggests an accident occurred, unable to verify. Woman insisted she hadn't been driving, that a 'Vivian' was driving. There was no indication of a 'Vivian' on the scene. Woman was taken to jail for DUI after blowing a 0.16 in breathalyzer. How do you want to plead?"

"Guilty. Let's get this over with," I said.

"Are you sure? You can fight it."

"No, it's not worth it."

"Okay, then plead 'no contest.' Don't worry, you won't go back to jail. They will suspend your license for one month. You will receive three years of informal probation, $1200 in fines, and eighty hours of community service. You will be ordered to attend twenty-five Alcoholics Anonymous classes, six months of alcohol abuse classes, three days of hospital and morgue classes, and you must complete a one-thousand word essay about your experience. The law also requires you install a breathalyzer in your car for six months. They will require you to pay for everything. It comes up to about $10,000."

"I was already fined $1000 from the city for my arrest! Are you sure I must go to the morgue? I have anxiety issues, I can't handle dead bodies!"

"It's standard unless you can get a doctor's note, but you can't drive while taking anti-anxiety medication, California has a zero tolerance for DUI offenders. Meaning within the next ten years, if you get pulled over and tested by a police officer, and they find any substance in your system at all, it counts as a second DUI. The judge will suspend your license today, do you have a ride home? An officer will watch when you leave to see if you drive. If you do, they will arrest you, so be careful."

I felt confused by what she read; I wasn't driving when the police arrived that night; I wasn't even in my car. And now the next several years of my life were ruined. I already worked seven days a week and couldn't afford my apartment as it was. Vivian contributed nothing financially, yet now I needed her more than ever!

"Let's go get some food! I'm starving!" Vivian said, when I returned to the courtroom.

"I can't eat anything, I'm too upset. Plus, I thought we would eat for free at

Happy Hills after?"

"The restaurant I was trying to take you to the night you went to jail, is across the street. I've been craving it since that day and been sitting here for hours for you Asterisk, I need lunch."

Defeated, I followed her out of the courthouse, across the street and into the diner. It was a walk up counter with a menu full of grease. Vivian placed her order and then stepped aside, assuming I was paying for her meal. I owed her for spending the day with me in court, so I handed over $17.

Vivian picked out our table. I told her what the public defender said. "You thought I was joking about them requiring the breathalyzer, Asterisk. Those things destroy the electrical in your car. It will never be the same. My friend told me he had to sell his car afterwards, the lights would flip on and off on their own. It was like it was possessed! Too bad you don't have a crappy car to install it in instead."

Just then the server dropped off Vivian's order. She had a large burger, a side of fries, a small side salad, a large drink, and an order of jalapeno poppers with ranch dressing.

"That's a lot of food!" I commented.

"I got these poppers for you. You have to try them. They are amazing!"

"I told you, my stomach is messed up. That would just make me shit myself in court."

"Whatever," she said, dunking one in ranch before stuffing it into her fat face.

I tore into her, "Vivian, I wasn't driving! The public defender said I wasn't even in the car! Where were you? Why did you leave me?"

"I already told you Asterisk, you punched me in the face so I took off."

"Why would you leave me like that? I would never, ever leave you."

"Violence is where I draw the line. You reminded me too much of my

160

psycho ex girlfriend that night."

"I WAS DRUNK! YOU SHOULD HAVE TAKEN CARE OF ME!"

"You are an adult, take responsibility for your own damn self."

I could see I was getting nowhere with her, the lunch recess was almost finished and I was desperate to get my time with the judge over with. As soon as court was back in session, it was my turn to take the stand. I plead "no contest" and took my punishment. They advised me to sign up for the alcohol classes that day.

It took less than an hour to complete the paperwork and transfer the classes to my county. It was getting dark, and I was eager to get home to Rosie. However, Vivian had her mind set on Happy Hills. Once inside the amusement park, we rode her favorite ride. Then true to her word, we walked up to the bar. It had been three months since I last had a sip of alcohol.

"An IPA please," I ordered.

"I must see your ID," the young girl at the counter said. I realized they had confiscated it at the time of the DUI, but remembered I still possessed my old one. I handed it to the bartender.

"Sorry, I can't serve you. It's expired."

"Oh, it's not really expired, I just lost my current one and until I get it replaced I'm using this as a backup."

"Sorry, park policy, I can't serve you without a current identification card."

I pulled off my sunglasses, "Look at me, I'm obviously old enough!"

"Come on Asterisk, let's go. A beer isn't that important," Vivian decided. We rode another coaster and then ate some food. Back at my SUV, Vivian revved the engine and took over my stereo, blasting horrible punk rock music from the 1990s. She drove like a maniac, honking and yelling at any car that got in her way. I gripped the door handle in fear.

"Can you slow down a little," I begged. "This is my new car and..."

"Don't tell me how to drive! At least you have a car!" I shut my mouth and prayed to the traffic Gods.

CHAPTER 27

After the stress from my court day diminished, the tension between Vivian and I vanished. She drove me to work every day and picked me up each night. I enjoyed having her company, though her maneuvering was scary and her choice in music was bleak. She kept the peace with Rosie, and they met me laughing and hungry that evening.

"Hey Asterisk, do you wanna grab a pizza for dinner? I asked Rosie already, and she said she's totally up to going to the joint with the arcade."

"That sounds great, but we can't afford it. We've been going out to eat way too often."

"Rosie was looking forward to it, but whatever. I told her if she was good we could go. Sorry Rosie, your mom doesn't want to get a pizza."

"Your manipulation is astounding. I hope you realize that I'm aware of what you are doing. It's fucked up."

Vivian made a sharp U-turn and drove toward our apartment. "Whatever

Asterisk. I don't need to eat tonight. That's fine."

Rosie's eyes filled with tears. Not in the mood for conflict, I shifted my stance, but I still had to set the ground rules. "Listen, we can go. But this is the only night we can eat out this week, I'm serious. Rent is due in six days and I'm still $1000 short."

"Fine." Vivian said. She turned the car around and headed towards the pizza parlor.

"Are we really going home?" Rosie asked, still sobbing.

"No, we will eat at the restaurant since you have been such a good girl."

We parked and walked inside. All eyes were on Vivian, she looked like a freak. She was wearing a long velour gown, chunky gray platforms and a face of foundation heavier than I wore in high school. Her lips were red and glittery, and her blush was at least an inch above her cheekbones. Again she had that bottom eyeliner drawn on like an advertisement for Crayola. Apparently, none of my beauty lessons had paid off.

I always supported the way she looked, but there were some nights I just wanted to hide behind a rock. This was one. She gripped my hand just long enough for everyone in the establishment to see we were together before she ditched me. Rosie ran to the arcade as Vivian found a booth to sit at while I waited in line to buy the food. I was getting used to it by now. After ordering, I joined Vivian at the table.

Rosie caught sight of me and charged over for a $5 bill. "Bring the quarters back here first, you can take two at a time. They are for games, not junk! I'm serious Rosie, don't come back with a bunch of cheap toys!" Two minutes later, Rosie returned with a plastic dog and a foot ball eraser wanting more quarters.

"What the fuck did your mom just tell you?" Vivian asked. Her voice carried so loud, that other patrons turned our way. I slouched into my seat.

"Rosie, I end up throwing them in the trash after a few days, anyway. Can you please play games instead?"

"No, the game I wanted to play cost six quarters, and you only gave me two."

"Fine, take six. But no more toys!" Rosie headed back to the arcade.

"You know she's manipulating you, right? You spoil that kid. She needs her ass kicked," Vivian lectured.

"Yeah, where do you think she's learning it?"

Vivian shrugged.

By the time dinner was over, Rosie had arms full of junk to carry to the car. As we made our way home, I got into my phone, and with her approval, signed Vivian up for food stamps. She qualified for $200 a month. I hoped that would save me the stress of being responsible for all her meals. She hadn't worked in months, and it wasn't from lack of effort. She wouldn't have been able to hold a job anyway, because I still needed her as my personal chauffeur until my driver's license suspension ended.

It was approximately 9:00 pm when we arrived home. Rosie was off to bed and out like a light. Vivian and I were snuggling on the couch, binge watching bad TV when it happened. "Babe, give me your hand," she ordered. Before I could acknowledge her request, she grabbed my arm and planted it on her crotch. It was rock solid. "I don't know why, but I'm really fucking horny right now!"

I wouldn't pass on that opportunity! "Remove your clothes," I ordered.

We both undressed, and I leaned into her, running my tongue down her stomach until I reached the base of her throbbing shaft. I peered into her eyes while slowly taking what was left of her manhood into my mouth. I sucked on her until she couldn't take it anymore, then we fucked hard and deep. When I could no longer hold myself back, I came, saturating us both. She continued thrusting until her estrogen melted arm muscles gave out, and she collapsed on top of me. "I can't get off this way."

Vivian rolled onto her back and stroked herself. I placed my lips around her left nipple and sucked. "Aww! That feels so good, suck my titty girl, help me finish." I continued to circle my tongue around her nipple as I

165

flicked the other with my fingernail. She released a tiny clear puddle onto her belly. "That's the most I've come in a year!" She wasn't fabricating, the female hormones had eliminated her sperm count. "I don't know what just happened, but I haven't had that sensation in a long time."

"It was magnificent!" I said.

"Yeah, well, don't get used to it... It's too bad we weren't dating before I came out, you would have loved it! I used to be hard like that every day." Her confession sent a tingle up through my crotch. "Tell me more!" I winked.

"I'm sorry to disappoint you, but I don't know if or when I'll feel that way again."

"It's okay, we'll find other ways."

CHAPTER 28

I t was fall, my favorite time of year. Well, it was until I realized I would not have Rosie for the upcoming four-day weekend. "Vivian, Rosie won't be here for Thanksgiving. What should we do?" I asked.

"Let's go to Happy Hills!"

"That drive isn't appealing, there will be tons of traffic."

"Then I don't know," she said.

"How about a brunch? Many local restaurants offer extravagant holiday menus and cooking at home will cost just as much."

"Fine. If you can locate one and you want to pay for it, we can go." I scoured the internet until I found a great brunch in a local restaurant I wanted to try. I sent the link over to Vivian and she agreed to accompany me, so I called in the reservation. The night before, Vivian mentioned that her friends had invited us to their place for Thanksgiving, "We can go after," she said.

The food was amazing and Vivian let me partake in some festive champagne. I practiced precaution and had just a glass. The food was incredible. After we stuffed ourselves on all you could eat turkey and side dishes, we headed to Vivian's friends' house. They greeted her warmly but insisted on using her "old" name and pronouns. I did my best to use her new name and female pronouns blatantly, but they didn't catch the hint. When Vivian's best friend offered me a beer, I looked to my lady love for permission, "Go ahead. It's a holiday." Just after dark, we said our goodbyes and headed home.

The day was a success and Vivian seemed proud of my controlled drinking. So two weeks later, when my birthday came around and I told Vivian I wanted to go to a brewery, she was okay with it. "I'm down! I'll drink some beers with you, girl! I know the perfect place." Vivian took us to a local spot we both wanted to check out. We each ordered some of their best sounding beers and played a board game.

On the way home, I mentioned to Vivian we should stop at the store for a six-pack. The night was young, and it was my special day. Vivian pulled off at our local grocery outlet and we both headed inside. Once to the beer isle, Vivian said something that surprised me. "I want to get hammered tonight! It's been a while. Wanna get fucked up with me, Five?" Really? Who did she think she was talking to? "Hell yes I do!" I shouted. This time, patrons turned around to gawk at me. I didn't care. I was with my favorite person in the universe, my kid was at her dad's for the weekend and I hadn't been slammed in months. Vivian grabbed two mammoth multi-packs of beer and layered them into a cart.

Yippee!

As soon as we arrived home, I rolled two joints while Vivian filled a trash bag with cans of the foamy liquid. Then we were off to another secret drinking spot. This particular one was atop of an abandoned pedestrian bridge over the freeway. We sat on the cool concrete as cars zoomed by below us in both directions. The rushing lights and cool breezes created a magical feeling. I opened a liquid refreshment for each of us, as Vivian lit a joint. I exchanged a beer for a hit of marijuana. We cuddled together and talked. Vivian told me a story about climbing into an abandoned building in her youth to drink like this, and I shared tales of my own. Before long, we were out of booze so we headed back to my apartment to reload our bag.

Our next stop was the bench by the lake. Vivian lit another joint, and I opened what was probably our ninth drink. Vivian was guzzling them down like a starving piglet latched onto her mom's tit. I watched as she crinkled the empty cans and threw them into the lake. "Stop doing that! The waste basket is right there." Vivian ignored me and I let it go.

The second bag didn't last any longer, so back to the apartment we went. By now it was past midnight, and I had about all the alcohol I could handle. Vivian also drank her limit. From the other room, I could make out the undeniable sound of regurgitation.

"BLEH! BLEH! BLEH!"

I ran into the kitchen to see Vivian crouched over my sink, chunks of puke were splattering everywhere. It reminded me of her in the shower with loogies or the Fourth of July. Why, she was a fireworks show of fluids. I couldn't help myself and drunkenly sang the Star-Spangled Banner.

"Bleeeehhhhh!"

"Oh, my God, Vivian, are you okay?" I asked. The sink was full of dishes, I contemplated asking her to relocate to the bathroom toilet, but didn't want to sound like a bitch.

After what seemed like forever, her sickness subsided. She rinsed out the sink and reached into the fridge and opened another beer. "You are on your own," I said, as I planted myself onto the sofa. I was passing out. My actions didn't slow Vivian down one bit, she was on a roll.

I woke up the next morning still on the couch, feeling more than a hangover. My chest was tight, and I had this weird sensation like I had to burp, but when I made myself, there wasn't any relief. The light on my phone was flickering, I picked it up and saw I had a voicemail from Vivian. That was odd, my phone dated it from 4:00 am. I hoped she was okay. Immediately, I called to listen.

"Hey girl, I know you are asleep and I hope you don't get this until later in the day so you can hear it and smile. I just wanted you to know that you are beautiful and I love you so much. You are fucking rad, Five. You are the coolest chick I ever met and happy fucking birthday! Happy birthday, girl! I'm at the lake right now drinking more beers. I drank thirty beers! The stars are beautiful tonight, just like your face. Anyway, I just wanted you to know how cool you are and how much I fucking love you Five. I hope you had a happy birthday! Get some rest girl. Tomorrow is gonna hurt. I love you, Five."

I rolled off the couch and stumbled into our bedroom to see my six foot sweet heart in her zebra panties curled up in the fetal position. I crawled into bed next to her, gave her a kiss and covered her with a blanket.

"I love you," I whispered.

"I love you too, Five."

CHAPTER 29

After a nap with my hungover princess, I awoke with extreme pressure in my chest. This wasn't the first time it had occurred, and I recognized it right away. I was in atrial fibrillation, my heart was only partially pumping blood, my body was weak and I had a huge bubble in my throat. I knew what had caused it, the binge drinking the night before. But, there was no way I would let Vivian know about it. It would just give her more ammunition. Besides, it usually went away on its own after a few hours. We spent the afternoon taking it easy; ordering takeout and watching murder mysteries. I continued to keep my ailment to myself hoping I would soon recover.

I had consumed part of a case of IPA already, trying to cure my hangover from the night before and take my mind off my medical condition. Rosie was outside running amok with the neighborhood kids.

Vivian had just finished smoking a bowl of chronic when our attention was diverted to the front door. It swung open with the force of a bowel movement from a Tyrannosaurus rex suffering from food poisoning. Rosie ran inside screaming. Her face was flushed and tears were streaming down her face.

"There is a woman chasing me!" she said.

"What are you talking about? Why? What did you do?" I asked.

"I was just playing with some friends. We found sticks and were using them as swords. This mean lady yelled at us and then grabbed my stick and said she would hit me with it! She is coming here to tell on me."

"God damn it, Rosie! Why were you playing with sticks to begin with? Did you hurt somebody? I buy you plenty of toys…"

Though she was stoned, Vivian bounced out of her hole in the sofa with the stealth of a ninja. "Some lady is trying to attack you? Is she out front? I need to see this shit!" Before I could stop them, both girls were outside. As I tried to maneuver my enormous ass off the couch, the shouting match began. I stumbled onto my front porch to see the strangest confrontation of my life.

Vivian was standing next to Rosie with her arms folded over her breasts. She was wearing a tank top covered in cat hair, a long wrinkled a-line skirt and rhinestone encrusted, pointy-toed flats. Spit was flying out of her mouth as she confronted the woman.

The woman looked like something out of a stereotypical 1970s sitcom and weighed somewhere close to 400lbs. She had dark skin and a head full of rollers. She was wearing a V-neck T-shirt with the sleeves cut off. The ripped left side hung so low you could see the top of one of her nipples peering out. Her breasts were so large and saggy they rested on her stomach. Grease stains marked her clothes, and she had on an old pair of slippers with holes around the big toes where her overgrown nails had pierced through.

Her entire body jiggled while she screamed. "Your kid is threatenin' me with this stick!" She held out a giant piece of wood so big, I was astonished my kid could have lifted it.

"Is that true, Rosie?" I asked.

"No! I was just playing with my friends! Then she came and stole it from me and said she would tell my parents."

Two kids Rosie's age riding Razor scooters pulled to a stop next to me. "Rosie is telling the truth! We were playing together and this crazy lady came over and took her stick for no reason! Then she threatened us!"

"You kids are all a bunch of liars!" the woman said.

"I think you are the liar, you disgusting slob!" Vivian yelled.

"Don't you call me no slob! You some pansy boy in a skirt!"

"I am not a 'boy'! I am transgender. But you are obviously too ignorant to know what that means. Go back to Compton where your trashy ass belongs!"

This was getting nasty way too fast for my liking.

"You a racist! I'm gonna make you my bitch!"

"Oh, you think you can make me your bitch? You are being prejudiced towards me! Go fuck yourself you dirty, fat hog!"

"I'm fittin' to take this stick and cram it up your ugly faggot ass!" the woman threatened.

"I'm not a faggot! I'm a lesbian!" Vivian yelled.

"Kids! Go home! Now! Rosie get in the house!" I screamed. It was bad enough, this happening at all, but I wasn't about to continue exposing the children to it.

"Why am I in trouble?" Rosie asked.

"I'm not saying anyone is in trouble. I just need all the kids out of here RIGHT NOW!" Rosie's friends whizzed away as she walked inside and slammed the door.

"You ain't no lesbian! You's got a dick. Let's see that thing!"

"You want to see in my pants? That's sexual harassment! You are sexually harassing me!"

I had had enough myself. I shook my head and left them there to duke it out on their own. Several minutes later, Vivian joined me inside.

"That woman was crazy!"

"Yes, I gathered that."

"She said she was going to make me her bitch'."

"I heard," I said, while flipping through the channels on the TV.

"I went to the office and complained about her! They said they know she's nuts! I hope they evict her!" Vivian said.

"Yeah, well, I hope you don't get us evicted by stirring up trouble."

"I didn't start it! She was being prejudiced! Besides, the office manager is gay. Gay men love me. There was no way he would take her side."

I went into the kitchen and grabbed us each a beer. Once things had settled down, I let Rosie play for the remainder of the afternoon with the condition she didn't pick up any more sticks.

Several hours later Rosie was in bed and the beer was gone. Vivian and I fooled around. "You want me to fuck you, Five?" she asked.

"Hell yes, I do!"

She climbed on top of me and inserted herself. After a few pumps she slowed down and started to snore.

"Vivian!"

"Huh?"

"Did you just fall asleep?" I asked, as the snoring resumed. I pushed her off me. "Wow! I'm so boring in bed that you can't even stay awake?" She groggily sat up. "Yes I can. Go get your vibrator."

I returned with a small toy and handed it to her. She rubbed it against me and then inserted it inside, while tickling my clit with her finger.

I awoke several hours later with a mouth like a desert and a full bladder. I grabbed a bottle of water and headed to the bathroom. I sat down and began to urinate.

PLOP!

Something had fallen into the toilet. I stood up and looked inside, only to realize that I had just given birth to my sex toy. I guessed we both had passed out.

The following day, I was still in atrial fibrillation. It was getting worse, but I sucked it up and headed to work anyway. A few hours in, I received a text from Vivian. "Asterisk, wanna go to a hockey game tonight? The tickets are cheap. Send me your credit card information so I can buy them for you and Rosie."

"I don't know, I think I may be in a-fib."

"What does that mean?"

"It means my heart isn't pumping right, but I'm okay, I just don't have a lot of energy and I need to rest."

"Do you mind if I take your car? I've been blowing my season tickets!"

"I guess so. Let me think about it, we might go."

"Think fast, they might sell out!" she predicted.

I completed my work, and although I wasn't any better; I didn't want Rosie to miss out at the chance of experiencing a hockey game. So, reluctantly I sent Vivian my credit card information. "We must head to the stadium straight from your work to make it on time."

"Can you grab me a clean outfit to wear?" I asked.

"Sure, what do you want!"

I messaged Vivian a list of what I needed a little while later, but she didn't respond. An hour passed before I tried texting her again, "Why aren't you getting back to me?"

"I'm doing my makeup. I want to be pretty for you. I packed your things, stop worrying."

I completed my workday and headed to the parking lot to find my car waiting. I climbed into the passenger side. Rosie was excited to see me and gave me a big hug from the back seat. Vivian handed me the bag of clothes. I looked inside to see she packed everything perfectly plus added something I had forgotten. That was the best part about dating a girl, she knew exactly what I needed. "You are awesome!" I said, giving her a big kiss. Her black lipstick smeared all over my face. "You look beautiful."

"Aww, thanks girl." Vivian grabbed my hand and held it until we merged onto the freeway. Once traffic let up, I dug through my belongings and quickly changed clothes. We arrived at the game in time to claim our tickets and make a quick stop at concessions before finding our seats. I bought Rosie the biggest bucket of nachos we had ever seen and a soda. Vivian ordered a pretzel with cheese as I picked up two enormous beers. I was hoping some alcohol might take the edge off my suffering. I should've been focused on eating something myself. An hour into the game I was buzzed and wanted to keep drinking. I grabbed us another round.

The game was almost over. "You need food!" Vivian said. "You are acting like a jerk. You keep kicking the chair in front of you. If that were me, I'd be pissed off!"

"I'm uncomfortable, these seats are too small!" I was having a hard time keeping still. My knees were jammed into my chest and I was having a difficult time breathing. I was ready to get out of there. The three of us left the stadium and headed back to the car. "Did you like the game, Rosie?" I asked.

"Yes! It was fun, Mommy. Are you okay?" Rosie could sense my pain. My face and ankles were swelling up.

"Yes, I'm fine."

"Your mom is fucking drunk!" Vivian yelled. "You need some food, Asterisk! You drank too much beer. Lucky for you, I know a great place down the street." Vivian parked my car in the lot of a Mexican restaurant. I was excited because Mexican food was my favorite cuisine! "Before you even ask, they don't sell margaritas, Asterisk. It's counter service."

"Damn it!"

Once inside, I realized there wasn't anything I could eat. Nothing looked remotely appetizing, and the building stunk. "Their al pastor is the best!" Vivian said.

"Yeah, well, I don't eat pork." I reminded her. They didn't even offer lard-free beans. My heart condition was worsening and the odor inside was making me nauseous. "I can't eat any of this." I handed Vivian a $20 bill and waited in the car. Vivian ate at the establishment so her dinner wouldn't get cold, instead of bringing it home. Sick and defeated, I passed out. I awoke just as Vivian pulled my SUV into our apartment complex. Exhausted, I stumbled my way through the front door. I didn't take the time to wash my face or remove my contact lenses, I bee-lined straight to my bedroom and hit the mattress.

The next morning I was still in atrial fibrillation. Again, I worked through it. Even though I needed to go to the hospital, I was reluctant because it would cost a million dollars. Unpaid hospital bills had already ruined my credit and I couldn't afford another one. The lack of blood flow caused my blood pressure to rise, and I spent the day with an extreme headache. I was glad when it finally ended.

"What are we doing for dinner tonight?" Vivian asked.

"I'm not feeling well. Just drive through somewhere."

"Yay!" Rosie yelled from the back seat. "I was worried about you last night, Mommy! You fell asleep in the car. I wanted to leave and take you home, but Vivian wanted to eat there. I kept running to the car to check on you and make sure you were breathing."

"Aww! You are so sweet. I was okay, you didn't have to worry like that,"

I said.

"Your mom wasn't sick, she was just drunk!" Vivian yelled.

"Shut up, Vivian! Don't teach her that."

"Yeah! Shut up, Vivian!" Rosie seconded.

"You shut up, Rosie!"

"Rosie, don't talk to adults that way! Vivian, don't talk to Rosie like that, she's just a kid." The argument wasn't any help to my already high blood pressure.

"She's a disrespectful little brat. You are lucky I'm not your mom, I'd beat your ass!"

"Enough!" I yelled. We sat in silence the rest of the way to the fast-food chain.

We made it home and Vivian turned on the TV. I sat next to her as we devoured our meal. After I finished, I curled up on her lap. I still wasn't getting any relief. "Can you rub my back?"

"No, I'm trying to watch this!"

"Please? I'm in pain and really uncomfortable!"

"Go for a walk," she suggested.

"Will you go with me?"

Vivian let out a sigh. "I guess."

I yanked on some sweatpants and my running shoes. Within minutes, we were outside. I needed to get my heart rate up. Maybe that would be the key to regaining a normal rhythm. "Walk faster!" I begged. "You go, I'll catch up," she said. I had to do something. This had gone on for too long. I was over being miserable, I had to get relief. I took off running as fast as I could. My feet pounded the pavement for half a mile until I collapsed on a grassy hill gasping for breath. I punched the left part of my chest with both fists and started to sob.

A few minutes later, Vivian was by my side. "Damn, girl! You really don't feel good, do you?" She was finally getting it. I shook my head. She pulled me up, put her arm around my neck, and walked me to the apartment. She rubbed my back for the remainder of the night. Her touch was soothing.

CHAPTER 30

On the fifth day of living with atrial fibrillation, I decided I could endure it no longer. "I'm calling out of work, can you take me to the doctor's this morning? I will see if they will prescribe me a different heart medication. I think that will help."

"What time?" Vivian asked.

"I don't know, let me make a call and see if they have any appointments available."

"You remember I start my new job at noon today, right?"

I let out a sigh, "Yes, but it's not clear how you can work that new job when we are sharing a car I can't drive!"

"I need to make money, Asterisk. I can't survive off you forever!"

"It's only for a few more weeks!" I reminded her. "Then I can install the breathalyzer and we can focus on buying you a vehicle... but fine. If you must start this job, I'll make sure I'm done on time."

I could get in at 9:30 that morning, and went in my pajamas, a hoodie and a pair of flip-flops. Vivian didn't look much better herself, wearing a pair of green and white striped men's shorts, sneakers and a band T-shirt. She hadn't bothered wearing a bra. I didn't have the energy to lecture her about indecency. Once to my appointment, Vivian pulled up near the entrance to let me out. "Aren't you coming in with me?" I asked.

"You know I don't like doctors' offices or hospitals, I don't want to get sick!"

"But I'm scared to go in alone."

"Ugh! Fine, if you really need me, I'll go!" She revved the car's engine to intimidate me. It worked; her anger caught me off guard. "Never mind."

"I'll be waiting for you next to that old tree. You'll be fine."

I climbed out and wandered the short distance to the building. There was a long line to check in. Once in the waiting area, they warned me there would be a fifteen minute delay. I shot Vivian a text to let her know. "Don't worry, I'll be out in plenty of time for you to get to work." After they called my name, I followed the nurse to a massive metal scale. Reluctantly, I stepped on. I looked away, deciding against any additional trauma. She sat me down and analyzed my blood pressure.

"Wow, that's high!"

"Yeah. I thought as much. I haven't been feeling well, I think I need to try a different heart medication."

"How long have you been on your current one?"

"About two years."

"Yes, it's time. The physician will prescribe you another type." She pulled out her stethoscope and listened to my heartbeat. Her face turned white. "Your heart doesn't sound normal. I think you might be in atrial fibrillation!"

"I know."

"Then why are you here? Why didn't you go to the emergency room?"

"Because it's expensive, and the last time I went, I was wrong. I can't afford to waste the money."

"How long has this been going on?"

"About five days."

"Oh, my God! You are officially my 'nightmare patient' of the month. The doctor will be in shortly to take an electrocardiogram of your heart."

After the EKG, they confirmed that I was in a-fib and directed me to the hospital. I walked outside and located my girlfriend. "Guess what?"

"You are in a-fib and need to go to the hospital. I figured as much, why didn't you go there to begin with, Asterisk? Must you go right now, or can it wait until tonight? I can't be late to my new job!"

"It's only a mile down the road. They said it's urgent. The doctor sent over my test results and they are expecting me. Can you drop me? I'll be there most of the day."

"Fine."

We headed towards the hospital. "While I was waiting for you, some dumb bitch flung her door open and dented your car. I would have gotten out and told her off, but she was breastfeeding a newborn. We made eye contact though, and I called her a stupid bitch. She got lucky."

"Great."

A few minutes later we arrived to the front entrance of the hospital. "Can you get out here?" Vivian asked.

"The emergency room is located on the back side. It's a big hospital, can you take me around?"

"Whatever, Asterisk. I'm just going to call out of work, this is getting ridiculous. I'll never make it there on time."

"You have an hour, Vivian. There isn't any traffic right now. You'll be fine," I comforted her.

"How will you get home?" she asked.

"I'll call an Uber."

Vivian all but pushed me out at the front entrance. I had to walk around the building to the emergency department. My tires squealed as she took off and I prayed she didn't wreck my car in her rush. I was admitted into the hospital and given a bed. However, the attending doctor didn't see my condition as urgent. "I talked to the heart specialist, and he said at your age it's a higher risk of stroke to cardio vert your heart back to a normal rhythm, then to let it do it by itself. If you would have come in within the twenty-four-hour window, we could have done it. At this point there's nothing I can do. The nurse will be in to release you shortly."

"What?" My mouth was agape. All these people just wanted my money! "I feel terrible! I can't work like this! I can't function!"

"I'm making you a follow-up appointment with your primary care physician."

"I just came from the damn doctor!"

His expression was blank.

After my discharge, I walked to the main entrance and ordered an Uber. I was halfway home when I received a phone call from Vivian. "Are you still at the hospital? I'm on my way, I'm coming to get you."

"No, they sent me home, I'm headed back to the apartment. What happened? Why aren't you working? Were you late?"

"No! The dumb manager didn't approve of my outfit! He said I was supposed to wear all black! He said he told me in the interview. He's such a liar, he never said that. I told him I'm homeless and I can't afford to buy new clothes!"

"So, can you come home and change? I'm sure there's something in my closet you can wear."

"No! They told me not to come back at all. The guy was a total dick."

"Jesus, well I guess this job wasn't meant to be."

Vivian's voice was drifting off, "I'll just see you at home."

CHAPTER 31

After visiting both the doctor and the hospital without receiving treatment, I had no choice but to take matters into my own hands. I modified my medication dosage on my own. I quit taking the pill that slowed my heart rate and doubled up on the blood thinners. Halfway through my sixth day of atrial fibrillation, I magically felt better.

It was now Saturday, my busiest time at work. I was eager to get caught up. Vivian seemed anxious too. We loaded into the front of the car, while Rosie climbed into the back. Vivian started the motor and her hideous hardcore music blasted through the speakers. It was only eight in the morning and I wasn't in the mood to tolerate it. Neither was Rosie, she had her hands cupped over her ears. I leaned forward and turned the stereo down a few notches.

"What the fuck?" Vivian shouted. "What's your problem?" Before I could explain, she had the volume up as high as it could go. Rosie screamed. I hit the "off" switch. "I have a headache. Put on something mellow."

"I'm sorry, I'm not like you Asterisk. I have taste in music. I don't listen to the same Lana Del Rey song every day."

"This is my car, and yet I let you play your crap every time you drive. Can you just give me some peace?"

"Fine. You want silence? You can fucking have it!" Vivian left the radio off and gave me the silent treatment the entire thirty miles to my job. At least, almost. We were about a block from the salon when it occurred.

As we reached a red light, a large white truck, towing a boat was attempting to cut through traffic and pull into a gas station. The man driving, inched carefully into our lane and waved at Vivian, as if to ask her permission. Vivian was not in the condition to be courteous and held down the horn. "Fuck you, asshole, get out of my way!"

"Vivian, stop it! It's a red light, let him pass!"

"You want to drive, you dumb bitch? Huh?" she asked. Before I could blink, she had the driver's side door open and was climbing out. She knew this would be the exact thing to draw in the police and have me arrested for violating my probation. All she had to do was get me behind the wheel.

"Vivian, knock it off. You are scaring us! You know I can't drive. Get back in the car, please."

"Then shut your mouth, cunt, and stop telling me how to drive. Fuck! I can't do anything right."

Rosie was crying. I did my best to soothe her while we merged onto the street leading into my job. I asked Vivian to pull over. Once stopped, I let her have it. "Get out."

"You want me to fucking leave? Yeah, I knew it. Well, I should just kill myself! Is that what you want? Im going to make you watch me kill myself right now!" Vivian jumped out of the car and ran into oncoming traffic.

"Rosie, don't look! Rest your chin on your knees!" Rosie obeyed. The rushing cars honked. One slammed on the brakes and skidded, barely avoiding her. I watched as Vivian, unscathed, disappeared into a shopping center.

"It's okay. You can pull your head up now," I told my daughter. "I'm sorry you had to experience that."

"Is Vivian okay?"

"Yes, she's just letting off steam."

I glanced at the clock. We were a half hour early. I debated what to do next. I knew I shouldn't drive. If they pulled me over, I'd go straight to jail and who knows what would happen to Rosie. I was sure a witness had reported the incident by now. I racked my brain. There must have been someone I could call to pick up Rosie but I couldn't think of anyone. I couldn't miss work either. Time ticked away as we sat together in silence.

Five minutes before my shift started, Vivian approached the SUV. "Can I come in?"

I unlocked the door. "Are you calm now?"

"I feel better," she said. Her face was a bright shade of pink and perspiration was dripping down her cheeks.

"I have to get to work but I'm afraid to leave you with Rosie."

"It'll be fine. I'm fine. I'm over it now," she said.

"What about you, Rosie?"

"It's okay, Mommy."

"I'm scared to leave you."

"I said we're fine! We are going to the beach to gather rocks. You wanna get some rocks don't you, Rosie?" Vivian asked.

"Yes," she answered. I only half believed her. Without another option, I left them together and headed into work.

Although I felt terrified for my kid, I sucked it up and played pretend for my clients. Vivian texted every few hours sending me pictures of Rosie on the beach, they eased my mind. Around 5:00 pm the girls picked me up.

They were starving but in good spirits. I took them to dinner at Rosie's favorite restaurant.

Once home, I asked them to join me for a walk to the lake. Well, Vivian and I walked, Rosie rode her scooter. My lady love and I were arm in arm, admiring the full moon, when Rosie rolled past. "Wahoo! Look what I have!" she yelled, holding up a small Styrofoam sword. "Rosie! I told you not to bring any toys!" As she swooped past a second time, I reached out and swiped her sword. "Here!" I tossed it over to Vivian, who had let go of my arm to play quarterback. She took the sword and ran like lightning. Rosie chased her, partially excited but still annoyed. Once she was close, Vivian threw it back to me. The game of "keep away" lasted several minutes until the toy ended up broken in half. Rosie put it in a trash bin voluntarily, because she was having fun.

"Let me ride your scooter!" Vivian teased my daughter.

"No way!"

"Aww come on!"

"Well, okay," Rosie said, coming to a stop next to my girlfriend.

"No, Vivian! You are too big, you will break it and I can't afford to replace it!"

"Fine!" Vivian pouted, crossing her arms over her chest. As we turned a corner, she vanished.

"Where did she go?" Rosie asked.

"She'll catch up."

I assumed, as she often did, that she was pissing behind a shrub like a guy. Several yards later, when she still hadn't returned, we crossed a bridge into the park. I kept my little one busy with small talk, but she was preoccupied with Vivian's whereabouts. After a quick circle we made it back over the bridge and Rosie screamed. "There she is!" But it wasn't Vivian, just a jogger.

"I bet she got tired and went home," I assured Rosie.

We were a block away from the apartment when we spotted her. She was sitting cross-legged in the middle of the sidewalk. She was such a creep. "What are you doing?" I asked, once we were in earshot.

She batted her eyes. "I assumed you two needed some 'mommy/daughter' time."

"Right."

I knew she was throwing another one of her tantrums, but I let this one go too. I was hoping to get Rosie to bed and try for a little action. The bitch owed me after the day she had put us through. Once Rosie was asleep and Vivian was in my bed wearing her g-string, I curled up beside her and kissed her neck. "No! Stop! Get off me! I'm not in the mood," she hissed. Insulted, I rolled over and fell asleep.

CHAPTER 32

Out of nowhere, Vivian's sex drive disappeared. The evening of her now famous erection was the last hurrah. It reminded me of a person dying from an incurable illness. The way they come alive and act fully recovered the day before their passing. Their loved ones get excited, thinking they are headed for recovery and then... Kaput! Sudden death. I shouldn't have been that surprised, after all that's what female hormones do, kill testosterone. Still, it was disappointing. Our sex life had been the best part of our relationship. "Asterisk, if you can get 'her' to work, then I'll try. I just can't feel much 'down there' anymore."

"We can do other things! I'll grind on you like a girl!" I made out with her and rubbed my pussy against her body, but that just made things uncomfortable. I massaged her breasts and sucked on her nipples. This time, not even a slight hint of an erection. So I did what I knew would work and went down on her. She became slightly hard for a moment, but by the end I gave up and accepted a quick hand job.

"At least you get off a hell of a lot easier than most girls," she confessed.

I figured I might as well stroke her ego since stroking the other thing didn't work. "It's because you are the best!"

"I know I am the best!" I should have seen that one coming.

As the days passed, I started my DUI and AA classes. Vivian had to escort me everywhere I went. Even though she drove like a jackass, I enjoyed knowing she was out there waiting for me. I don't think she liked it as much. Actually, I'm sure she resented me for it.

One thing I knew Vivian loved as much as life itself was food. I think she appreciated it more than I did hooch! Since sex was no longer a viable option, the two of us dove into our other favorite pastimes. Each night after work, we would pick a new restaurant. I would indulge in their craft beer selections, while Vivian gobbled up everything fried. Within a month we both looked like washed up porpoises.

Whenever I tried to get in her pants, or if I passed out too early for her liking, Vivian would criticize me. "You act like a gross, drunken pig." I'm not sure if she recognized she was mutating into the same pig, as she could no longer fit into her boy shorts and her chin had all but disappeared. We were both trapped in this together! At least for another week...

I had an appointment to install a breathalyzer in my car; you know 'the ole blow and go'. It was a device used to test the alcohol content in the breath of a driver, installed within the electrical equipment of a vehicle. Basically, if the device found any trace of liquor, the engine would lock the driver out. They would have to tow the car to a mechanic for a reset and pay another hefty fine to the state. Yippie! As much as it sucked, it meant I would get my freedom back from Vivian and her bad music. I must admit, I was eager to have my driving privileges reinstated while my car was still in one piece.

Vivian dropped me off at work one weekday morning prior to my installation and kissed me goodbye. "Have a good day, hun!" She was in a great mood because she had another job interview. I was feeling much better since my atrial fibrillation had passed. A few hours into my workday, I received a text from Vivian. "I've got a second interview! They really liked me!"

"That's wonderful! Let's go out to celebrate. I made a lot of money and have such a positive feeling about our futures. Everything will work out now, you'll see!"

Vivian picked me up that night with Rosie in the back seat. The three of us pigged out at dinner. We were on our way back to the apartment when I asked Vivian if we could stop at a brewery for another round. "This may be the last time we can go out and have a beer together before that ridiculous device gets installed. I bet Rosie would like to play some board games."

"Yeah, that sounds fun! Let's head home real quick and grab the growlers."

"Great idea!" I said.

We were just a block away from the apartment when Vivian teared up. "What's the matter, sweetie?" I asked.

She shook her head. "I can't tell you."

"Oh, my God, are you crying? What's wrong?"

"You are going to be really upset."

"Look Vivian, if you cheated on me, I don't want to know."

"It's not that..." Her crying was now 'B movie' material. Tears encased with black mascara cascaded down her sparkly cheeks.

"It's my car, you hit someone, didn't you?"

"Mm-hm."

Vivian pulled into my garage. "When?"

"This morning, on my way to the interview."

"Why didn't you tell me earlier?" I asked.

"Because you were having such a good day, I didn't want to ruin it!"

When she put the car in 'park', I scrambled out to assess the damage. Even though the accident was on my side, I hadn't noticed because it was dark out. I was seeing the smashed in fender for the first time. "Whose fault was it?" I asked. I already expected the answer. "Hers, but they will blame me because her car was hit from behind. It wasn't my fault, Asterisk! The dumb bitch pulled out in front of me and stopped short. You are lucky I pulled your emergency brake, it could have been worse! They'll still blame me. Insurance companies are idiots."

I stormed into the house, plopped my lumpy ass on the couch and crossed my arms under my breasts. Vivian and Rosie followed behind me. "Do you still want to go to the brewery?" Vivian asked. I gave her "the death stare."

"No! Our evening is over. Rosie get in the bath. Vivian don't talk to me. I'm going to bed."

Vivian cried crocodile tears most of the night. The next morning she filed the claim. "The guy was such a douche! He couldn't figure out who he was talking to! He kept calling me John, I told him my name was Vivian, like five times! Then he addressed me by 'sir', I told him, 'I'm not a man!' Fucking idiot!" Vivian was proud of herself for confusing the poor guy.

"Vivian, if the insurance company doesn't know who you are then they won't cover the accident and I'll be responsible to pay it out of pocket!" I opened up the insurance application on my phone and sure enough the name on the report was "Vivian Johnson", not "John Henderson." I emailed my insurance agent right away explaining John was in fact Vivian. I was not nearly as "amused" by this mistake as Vivian seemed to be.

CHAPTER 33

It was the morning before Valentine's day. I had an enormous work load but still needed to get my breathalyzer installed. "I guess I'll just have to call out," I told Vivian. I was struggling to juggle my career, the house, motherhood, our relationship and my court order. "No, go to your job. I'll take the car for you," she offered. "Really? You would do that?" Her unselfishness was out of character. "Yes. We need the money and it's not like I have anything better to do. It will take most of the day, anyway."

"I love you!" I said, reaching over and giving her a giant hug.

"No problem, Five." Vivian drove me to work and then as promised, took my car to the mechanic. Halfway through she sent a text. "These guys seem cool, but the device you ordered is a piece of shit. They can't get it installed right."

"Crap, how much longer is it going to take?"

"They said it should be done by closing."

"When is that?" I asked.

"6:00 pm."

"I'll be finished at 4:00, but I can wait."

"I'm so fucking bored, Five! You owe me!"

"Thank you, I really appreciate your help." I continued working until my last client left, and I sent Vivian a text. "I'm all done! How's it going your way?"

"They aren't gonna finish it today."

"What? Are you serious?"

"Yeah. You have to take it back on Monday. They should have the car put together soon and then I'll head out."

I sat around for an hour and with little else to do; I helped myself to a glass of wine. I always had a few bottles in the mini fridge for customers. It took the edge off waiting. It was nearing 6:00 pm, and I hadn't heard back from Vivian. I shot her another text. "Any news?"

"Just left, but it may be awhile with traffic."

"Seriously?" I asked.

"Don't get bitchy with me! I sat in a hot ass mechanic's office all day for you! I was bored as fuck, my phone is almost dead and I haven't eaten all day!"

"Just get here when you can. I'll take you to dinner anywhere you want. I love you!" I figured I had better send Rosie a text since we would be home late.

"Rosie, my car is taking a long time at the mechanic, so we won't be back for a while. Can you heat a frozen meal for yourself?"

"Yes, Mommy, but will you get me Valentine's day cards to give out at school tomorrow?"

Holy crap! I had totally forgotten. "Yes, and I'll pick up some candies too.

Text me the kind you want."

"Thanks, Mommy."

I still had time to kill, so I poured myself a second glass and opened up a magazine. Vivian messaged when she was close. I cleaned up the back room and headed outside to the parking lot. Vivian pulled up right away, and I climbed in.

"See this thing!" she said while holding up what resembled a giant electronic cigarette box. "You have to blow in it really hard, and I mean, really hard. I don't know if you can do it! It's not working correctly. They said they would adjust it next week when you go back. It should be easier to use once they fix it." We pulled out onto the street and it chimed for the first time.

"You have to blow into it to start the car, and again when it randomly beeps as you drive. I have to do it again. Here we go!" I watched as she put the device inside her hot pink lips and blew with all her might. The breathalyzer continued to beep. Her cheeks puffed up and turned red. Suddenly she stopped blowing and sucked with her mouth still around it. She sucked so hard I thought she might swallow her cheeks. Without removing the device, she let out a second blow with such force, her eyes looked like they might bulge out of her lash extensions. "You want to try it next?"

"No. It's okay. I'll wait until tomorrow."

"You are gonna do it next!" she insisted.

"I can't."

"Why not?" she asked.

"I had a glass of wine while I was waiting for you."

Vivian shook her head.

"What do you want to eat? I'll take you anywhere."

"Pasta Garden."

"Fine with me, it's close to home."

Vivian blasted some outdated ska and drove like a madwoman. The accident hadn't taught her anything. Twenty minutes later we were strolling into the restaurant. "Table for two, please," I said.

The hostess glanced at her computer, "There's a thirty-minute wait. Here's a buzzer and a bar menu. All beer and wine are half off until your table is ready." I took them from her and before I could say "thank you," Vivian ripped them right out of my hand. "I don't fucking think so!" she shouted, sounding like a counselor at a fat camp. "This bitch has a DUI! I just spent the entire day having her breathalyzer installed! Fuck no she isn't having more wine!" I spun around on my heels, handed the buzzer back to the hostess and declared, "I don't deserve this shit."

I stormed out leaving Vivian there alone. It was raining, so I went into my car, grabbed my umbrella from under the seat and began the trek home. Seeing a lit sign for a grocery store a block later, I remembered my promise to Rosie. I hustled inside and bought the cards and candy she asked for. Once I paid the clerk, I left the store and continued on my journey. Another block later I felt my phone buzz. It was a text from Vivian. "Where the fuck are you?" I ignored it and passed a few streets. That's when it started.

An engine revved, followed by the sound of squealing tires. "What the fuck are you doing? I thought we were having dinner?" I didn't acknowledge her. "Get in the car, Asterisk! It's raining, are you fucking crazy?"

"I have an umbrella, I'm fine." Vivian followed me half a block, then rolled up the window and took off. I kept going. A few minutes later I heard the screeching tires again and turned in time to see the car sliding on the wet pavement. This time Vivian left it running in the middle of the street and approached me. She was centimeters from my face. "What the fuck is your problem? I sat at the mechanic all day for you, and this is how you treat me? Get in the fucking car, bitch!" Her spit stung my face as she screamed.

"No thanks. I'm fine walking. I'll meet you at home."

"You are such a stubborn cunt! Get in! Get in the car now!" I held back my sobs, noticing a man on a bicycle watching us. I prayed he wouldn't call the cops, knowing I had the smell of alcohol still on my breath from earlier. Vivian spotted him too. She hopped in the vehicle and sped away. I was just a few signals from home, praying to the universe I would make it.

A few minutes later Vivian returned, she rolled down a window. "I want you to know you are a fucking bitch, Asterisk. I am hungry. You brought this on yourself! I'm going home to pack my things and I'm leaving you. I'm over your bullshit!" I ignored her and continued walking. The man on the bike rode over to me, "Are you okay?"

"Yes. I'm fine. Thank you." He nodded, then followed me the rest of the way home. I was grateful. Fifteen feet from the apartment entrance I spotted a police car as it drove towards me. "Please don't stop. Please don't stop," I whispered as he rolled past.

Once inside my apartment, Rosie greeted me. "Did you get my Valentine's day cards, Mommy?"

"Of course," I said, handing her the wet bag. Just then the front door swung open. "Your mom is a fucking cunt!" Vivian yelled. "Rosie, go sign your Valentine's in your room, okay?" I said. "Shut your door!"

"Fuck you, Asterisk! You bitch! I can't believe you pulled this shit tonight!"

"You are abusing me, Vivian, I don't deserve this."

"You are the abuser! You punched me! Remember? Never forget that you were the one who hit me!"

"I don't even recall the incident, but if I did, I'm glad! I'm sure you deserved it. You are lucky I don't punch you now!"

"I'm moving out of here! I can't take your shit anymore!"

"Great!" I said, showing a toothy smile. "When?"

"As soon as I can, I'm serious. You are on your own."

"Awesome!"

Vivian marched into our bedroom and slammed the door.

CHAPTER 34

The morning of Valentine's Day I readied myself for work. "I have to take off in twenty minutes," I told Vivian. She ignored me. "Will you drive me or should I call an Uber?"

"Ugh. I'll take you," she said.

"Thank you."

I climbed into my car and was caught off guard by the stench. It was a mix of onion and garlic that reminded me of a vampire hunt. "What is that smell?" I asked.

"I don't know," Vivian said. I glanced to the floor and saw the buzzer from Pasta Garden resting near my feet. I picked it up and put it to my nose. That explained it.

"You stole this?"

"So what? I'm sure it happens all the time."

The ride to work was quiet. Vivian didn't say another word to me nor did she turn on the music. She dropped me off, and I ventured inside. It was hectic at the salon. My clientele all wanted to look nice for an evening out with their special someone. I worked until 7:00 pm. I messaged Vivian an hour before my shift ended to let her know when I would be ready. She showed up five minutes late. I got in the car and buckled my seat belt.

"How was your day?" she asked.

"Shitty." I had my pants rolled up to my knees, and a pair of soggy shoes in hand. "A pipe burst and the salon flooded. Nobody bothered to help me clean it up. I'm soaking wet." I looked like I had just crawled out of a washing machine. "I'm sorry, hun. Here!" she said, handing me a small plastic container. "I got you something."

"Thank you." I rested it on my lap but didn't peer inside. "Do you like those?" Vivian asked. "I bought them for you with my food stamps. They were expensive." I glanced in the box to see six giant chocolate covered strawberries. "These usually are. Thanks."

We drove the rest of the way without speaking. It was quiet when we arrived home. I was grateful that Rosie had gone to her dad's for the weekend. I stripped off my wet clothes and hopped in the shower. Afterwards I put on my pajamas and entered the living room to find Vivian planted on the sofa in her purple panties, zoning out to reality TV.

I opened the fridge, surpassing my valentine's gift, and clutched a full bottle of rose'. I poured myself a giant glass and carried the bottle with me as I joined her on the couch. She filled me in on the story she was watching. I let yesterday's argument go. Soon I was feeling relaxed but realized I had finished my wine.

I sneaked back to the fridge and discovered two stray IPAs left from the weekend before. I opened one and took it with me to my seat. I scooted close to Vivian and put my palm on her thigh. I was testing the waters. After a few seconds, I slid it up to her crotch. "Stop!" she slapped my hand. "You are sloppy when you are drunk. I'm going to bed."

I blankly stared at the television for a while, reliving the events from the night before while I finished my beer. The more I thought about it, the angrier I became. So when the recollection of Vivian's dagger surfaced, I constructed a plan of revenge. I crept into our room and while she was snoring, reached under the bed and dragged the knife out of its hiding place. I decided that Vivian had been cruel to me for the last time. I was ready to cut a bitch. That's right! I would stab her in the gut with her own weapon. I examined it, then tried to remove it from the leather case. I fumbled with the buckle for several minutes but couldn't get it undone. I was too drunk to figure out how to unlock it. Vivian thought my being intoxicated was a bad thing, but little did she know it just saved her life. I put the knife away. Though I had been defeated at slaughtering my tranny pig, I still needed blood. I stumbled into the bathroom, removed a blade out of my disposable razor and sliced it down my left arm. I continued cutting until my triceps resembled a drawing done by a three-year-old.

When I finished, I went back to bed and attempted to push Vivian awake.

"Vivian, Vivian, I cut my arm," I said.

"Huh?"

"I cut my arm. It's bleeding."

"I'm sorry. Go to sleep."

I crawled into bed with her and fell asleep with my leg pressed against hers.

CHAPTER 35

I awoke the following morning cuddled up to Vivian. My mouth was dry and I could already sense a headache coming on. I reached over the side of my bed to grab a bottle of water. I put it to my mouth and chugged.

"What the hell, Asterisk?"

"Huh?"

"There's blood everywhere! What happened to your arm?"

Until she said that, I had forgotten about the night before. Now intense stinging radiated through my open wounds. I examined my injuries; they were humongous. "I fell," I lied.

"You fell on what? Barbed wire?"

"I was walking down the stairs to check the mail, and I slipped, my arm scraped the stucco. It sure felt like barbed wire."

"Ew. Go clean it up! Put some peroxide on it or something. This is almost as messy as sex is during your period."

Even though it was a bad lie, Vivian bought it, or at least she pretended that she did. I regretted what I had done. I flashed back to myself holding the blade in my hand and was grateful I hadn't been able to access it. Vivian rolled out of bed and walked into the bathroom. A second later I heard the water turn on. I knew she would be in there at least an hour, so as I often did, I joined her. "Hey, baby girl," she said.

Vivian took the shower head off the stand and rinsed me off. "You need to be careful. I don't know how you party so hard. I worry about you. You will kill yourself if you keep drinking like that."

"I'm fine!" I insisted. Vivian grabbed a bar of soap and scrubbed my body with it. I was over ran with guilt. "You know that knife you hid under the bed?"

"Yeah. What about it?" she asked.

"Find a better place to hide it."

With that I slipped out of the shower and into a towel before entering the bedroom closet. I needed to find something to wear that would cover my wounds. I decided the giant blue hoodie Vivian drunkenly encouraged me to buy at Happy Hills would do.

I dressed before Vivian was done. Eventually she was ready to leave. She resembled a boy, wearing a band T-shirt and knee-length shorts.

Today she was cashing in the first part of her laser hair removal voucher I bought her months ago. I tagged along. Not just because I was interested, but I knew how uncomfortable Vivian was in situations like this and I figured she could use my support.

We pulled into the parking lot and Vivian grabbed my hand as we entered the building. The waiting room was fairly small with a large glass window in the front which didn't allow for privacy. Several women were already there filling up the empty seats. We waited in a short line. When it was our turn, Vivian addressed the lady working the front desk. "I have an appointment for Vivian Henderson."

"Let me see," we watched as she scrolled through a computer. "Here we go, 'full facial laser'. Can you sign this waiver please, Vivian?" She tried handing the clipboard to me.

"She's Vivian," I said with a brow raise, passing the paperwork to my girlfriend. The woman turned red. I felt bad for both of them. Vivian didn't look feminine today, but it still pissed her off. The receptionist seemed embarrassed and confused. Vivian turned in the clipboard and a few minutes later, they called her name. I accompanied her into the treatment room and was handed a pair of tinted goggles to wear so I could watch the procedure.

"It will hurt the most on the dark areas," the technician warned. Once my girlfriend was resting on the bed with her arms crossed over her shoulders like a corpse, the nurse went to work. I could hear the hair sizzle as she zapped Vivian's face and then I could smell it. It must have been painful because after each zap, Vivian would let out a grunt and grab the sides of the cot. She kicked her feet and turned her hips, yet managed not to move her head. That bitch was determined; pain or not, she would rid her cheeks of that damn stubble, once and for all!

I was in hog heaven. Watching Vivian getting tortured was the medicine I needed all along.

ZAP! "Gah!" ZAP! "Ahh!"

"Ha hahaha!" I giggled.

"Stop laughing, Asterisk," she mumbled between clenched teeth. Vivian shrieked. "Can you go over that spot again?" I asked. The three-minute session didn't last long enough. My lady lumps didn't share my opinion.

When it was over they sent us into a bathroom. Vivian was instructed to apply aloe vera lotion onto her face. "Here, you do it for me!" she ordered. I washed my hands before filling them with the cool gel. "Okay. Come here," I said. Vivian inched in close to me and I gently applied the solution to her charred cheeks.

"You enjoyed that, didn't you?"

"Oh, you have no idea!"

As we were walking to the car, I decided I had to come clean. "I have to tell you something. Last night, I didn't fall."

"I kinda figured that, hun. What really happened?"

"I cut myself," I said.

"Why did you do that? What did you use?"

I shrugged. "My bathroom razor."

Vivian rolled her eyes. "Girl, you gotta chill out."

CHAPTER 36

I t was Monday morning, and I had taken the day off to finish the installation of my breathalyzer. I peered at the clock. My appointment wasn't for another two hours. I slipped my hand under the blanket and onto Vivian's nipple. I squeezed it just how she liked. When she moaned, I immediately became wet. She ran her hand onto my breast, following my lead. I reached for her "clit" and rubbed. Vivian reciprocated, smoothly sliding her index finger in and out of me. Even though she wasn't becoming erect, she continued. She was great with her hand and it didn't take long for me to come close to orgasm.

"You feel so good! Don't stop!"

"You like that, baby?" she asked. "Does that feel good?"

"Yes! Oh, my God, I'm almost there! Put another finger in!"

"No."

"What? Give me another finger! I'm about to finish!"

"I don't want to."

"What? What do you mean? Just... just do it! Please!"

"You never had a problem with my hand jobs before!"

Then I came, but just barely. I sat up, "What the hell, Vivian?"

"What?"

"Why wouldn't you give me two fingers?"

"I didn't feel like it."

"You can't just 'not feel like it!' It was my orgasm!"

"I don't know why you are making this into such a big deal. Get ready, we have to leave soon." Vivian stood up and left the bedroom. It pissed me off, but I joined her in the shower anyway. As usual, I was clean long before she got out.

We made it to the appointment on time. Lucky for me the mechanic was across the street from the Department of Motor Vehicles. "Take this paperwork next door while we complete the installation. When you finish, your car should be ready," the operator said.

Although the DMV was my least favorite place to go, the prospect of receiving my driver's license back excited me. I hadn't driven in almost four months. The entire application process only took an hour. I couldn't believe it. I told the clerk, "This is more exciting than when I got it the first time!"

After settling the fee, Vivian and I returned to check on the status of my vehicle. "It's all done. Sign here and you will be on your way." After signing my name, the technician walked me through the blowing process. Once I had been successful, we were off!

I headed in the freeway's direction. Twenty feet from the on-ramp, the car stalled. "Great! Just great!" I screamed. The breathalyzer let me blow into it again, and it started.

"Turn around Asterisk, there's something wrong."

We drove back to the mechanic and sure enough; they had to work on my car again. "There are four possible ports for us to use. Since every machine is different, there isn't a manual. We just have to try each one until we get it right. Unfortunately, we have to open your car up and then put it back together each time we try. This was the second port. I'm confident we will have it right next time, the odds are in our favor. Have a seat inside and wait," the technician said.

"Is there a place good to eat within walking distance?" I asked. I could tell Vivian was starving and after the last time, I knew how this could end. "The diner down the street is fantastic!" We ate at the restaurant for lunch but it only killed about forty-five minutes. Afterwards we returned to the mechanic. Try as they might, it still took the rest of the day to get the breathalyzer installed. Vivian was out of patience. It was already getting dark by the time they finished.

We left as they were closing for the night. Flying down the freeway, I turned to Vivian. "It's great to have my freedom back!" That's when I realized I could play my choice of music, so I turned it on. "You won't be driving my car ever again, Vivian. I don't have to put up with you treating me like shit anymore either!" I laughed.

Vivian gave me an evil glare and turned her head to look out the window. Before going home, I stopped at the local grocery store. Vivian opened her door and followed me inside without saying a word. I grabbed a basket and started down the first isle. "Vivian, what looks good to you?" I asked, while we were standing near a wall of snacks. Vivian was giving me the silent treatment. She had her phone out and was busy texting somebody else.

I pretended I didn't notice and shopped on my own. Several minutes later I asked, "When I enter the checkout lane, can you grab a case of water? I don't have room for it in the cart." Vivian didn't acknowledge my request and instead wandered away. I didn't see her again until I was already in line with a full basket. "Can you go grab the water now?"

"I already picked up a case of water! I carried it around the entire store looking for you but you were nowhere to be found! Go get your own fucking water! I'm not your slave!" she shouted. I chose not to react and skipped the water. It wasn't worth it.

Once I paid, and they bagged the food, I pushed the cart to my car. I unpacked everything into the trunk while Vivian wandered the parking lot. When I finished, I motioned for her to come towards me with my finger. Once she was close, I pulled her to me by her collar. "Don't you fucking act that way in public ever again! Do you understand me? I'm not tolerating your shit anymore."

"What?" she yelled. "I didn't do anything!"

"Get in the car and keep your voice down."

When we arrived back home, Vivian ran inside and took a seat at the kitchen table. She chose not to help carry in the groceries. After putting everything away, I glanced around the apartment. She had destroyed it. Her makeup, weed and dirty clothes were scattered everywhere. The sink was full of her used dishes. "You need to tidy up after yourself! I already pay all the fucking bills. The least you can do is pick up around here!"

She didn't look up from her phone. "You are going nuts, Asterisk. Calm your shit."

"You won't even give me two fingers!"

Vivian rolled her eyes.

"You want to be a woman? Well, women clean!" I continued.

"I'm not good at cleaning."

"Learn!" I picked up her soiled clothes and threw them in the hamper.

She reached for her bong and took a hit. That was the straw that broke the camel's back. "You know what Vivian? You will never be a woman. No matter how hard you try! You will never pass as female!" I regretted the words the minute they came out of my mouth. "I know," she replied without showing emotion. I watched as she reloaded her bong. After she took a second hit, I ran into the bedroom, flung my body onto my bed, and cried myself to sleep.

CHAPTER 37

After having witnessed Vivian's worsening behaviors, Rosie mimicked them. Or perhaps it was her passage into becoming a tween. All I know is that one night I put my sweet little baby to bed and the next day, out arose a teenager.

"You need to brush your hair, Rosie." I reminded her, one morning before school. She stomped into the bathroom as hard as her giant feet would allow. She yanked open a drawer with such force, the entire thing hit the floor causing my makeup to scatter. "Seriously?" I asked. I accompanied her inside and picked up the wreckage. "Try to calm down or you will make yourself late again!"

I observed as my child ferociously brushed her hair; she was ripping out strands and shrieking. "You are hurting yourself, be gentle," I begged. She ignored me and stomped away.

"What the fuck is going on?" Vivian shouted. "I'm trying to sleep!"

"Rosie is having a tantrum, I'll handle it, try to get some rest." I shut the bedroom door and headed into the kitchen where my daughter was now standing. She had an evil smile pasted across her face.

"There!" she said, pointing to the ground. "Are you happy now?" A huge chunk of Rosie's blond curls sat on the tile. She was gripping a pair of scissors.

"Wow!" I said. "Turn around." When she did, I could see her scalp. She removed most of the length from the back of her hair leaving a giant hole. "Go to school. When you get home, I'm shaving your head. There's no way to fix that. You have been growing it out for so long, I can't believe you would do that to yourself."

"This is what you wanted! You told me to take the knots out, and now they are gone!" I watched Rosie pick up her backpack. She put it on and slammed the front door as hard as she could on her way out. The windows rattled.

I scooped up the hair from the floor. Just as I was about to throw it in the trash, Vivian wandered into the kitchen. She was wearing a see-through pair of fishnet panties. While taking a bottle of water from the refrigerator she noticed the chunk of hair in my hand. "What the hell?"

"Rosie threw a tantrum and gave herself a trim."

"Your kid is a brat. Girls don't do that. I told you she's really a boy."

"Stop it!"

When Rosie arrived home that afternoon, she had the hood of her sweatshirt up, hiding the back of her hair. "How was your day?" I asked. "Fine. My friend said she'll let me borrow a wig." Rosie took her backpack off and threw it onto the floor. "If you shave my head, I'll do something mean to you! My friend helped me come up with a plan."

"Well, I considered it, and the worst punishment is to let you live like that. I'm not going to cut your hair. You can walk around with that giant hole for now on."

"Fine!" she stomped into her room, slamming the door.

As the days passed, the fits of rage escalated until Rosie had battered the door off its hinges. I tried everything I could to get her to behave. I took away her phone and grounded her from playing outside. When that didn't work, I tried the contrary and rewarded her good behaviors. That approach made matters worse between Vivian and me.

"You spoil that kid. She needs to be beat! I don't know why you had her door repaired, I would have left it off permanently. If I treated my mom the way Rosie treats you, I'd have gotten the shit beat out of me. Actually, I did and for much less. You are a good mom, she doesn't deserve you. Send her to live with her dad."

"I think it's the hormones, Vivian. I need to get them checked again. Maybe she's having a rush of testosterone. I'm calling the counselor."

"When I was her age, I didn't act that way. I wouldn't have cut my hair off, had my mother allowed me to grow it. She caught me dressing in her clothes once and went crazy. Rosie is lucky to have a mom that supports her. I used to hide in the bathroom with the water running for hours doing my makeup, just to wash it off."

"I bet they didn't have a clue! Ha haha!"

"Nope! They thought I was doing what all teenage boys do, but I wasn't! Makeup and being a woman were way too important to me. I see none of that in Rosie."

"Everyone is different," I reminded her.

CHAPTER 38

V ivian had another job interview that afternoon. Although I had told her I wouldn't allow her to drive my car anymore, I didn't see a way around it. The interview was halfway through my workday and I was eager for her to get back on her feet and out of our home. "It's a nice day, Asterisk. When I finish, I'll take Rosie down to the beach for some exercise." Reluctantly, I handed over my keys.

Vivian arrived to pick me up from my job that evening with Rosie pouting in the back seat. "What's going on?" I asked, already feeling the tension between them. Rosie had her arms crossed over her chest and tears were streaming down her cheeks. Vivian's eyes were protruding out of their sockets, and her lipstick was smudged. I could feel her body shuddering with rage. "Your kid is a psycho little bitch!"

"Whoa! No, no! You can't talk about Rosie that way. Vivian, that is not okay."

"You don't even fucking know what she did and you are already taking her side!"

"I'm not picking sides by telling you not to verbally assault Rosie."

"You are always on her side!" she continued, as we merged onto the freeway. "I took your brat daughter down to the beach to collect rocks. She wanted to bring back a giant stone she couldn't even carry. I told her, 'No way, your mom won't allow that.' Then she picked up a handful of pebbles and threw them at a stranger's car! She scratched his paint! So, I told her, 'Get in the SUV, we are leaving.' She not only refused, but she opened your door and slammed it so hard I thought she broke the latch. I've heard nothing so loud in my life, my ears are still ringing."

"Rosie, why do you think this behavior is okay? Vivian took you to the beach. She didn't have to do that! You should be at home studying. Your grades have been dreadful. Empty your pockets!" I ordered. She looked out the window, "I said empty your fucking pockets!" Rosie gave me the evil eye, as she reached inside and handed over the contraband.

"Now, can we get dinner, please? I haven't eaten all day."

Vivian pulled into a local pizza restaurant that lacked an arcade and sat down to order. Taking advantage of my designated driver, I started off with an IPA. Vivian ordered a coke. Rosie wanted nothing. "I hate this place. I'm not eating," she declared. "Great. It will be cheaper," I said.

Vivian didn't have many words for me either. She was still mad I hadn't taken her side. We ate most of our meal in silence. At the end, Rosie grabbed several slices of pizza and scarfed them down.

Once home, I told my daughter to shower and get into bed. She protested. Instead of turning on the water, and cleaning herself as I had asked, she stomped into the bedroom and screamed at the top of her lungs. Her fists were clenched at her sides.

"Ahh! Ahh! Ahh!"

"Rosie, stop that! This type of behavior is unacceptable."

I watched in horror as she pounded on the walls. She didn't stop until her knuckles were bloody. In pain, she threw her toys around the room while stomping her feet. I had never seen a tantrum like it. I went to her side, attempting to do some damage control. Instead, she knocked me to the ground. I pulled myself up only to have her slam her door on me, trapping my hand. I screamed out in pain.

Vivian ran to my side, "What's going on?" "Rosie slammed my arm in the door! Rosie if you broke my hand, I won't be able to work!" Vivian used her body to push the door open, freeing my wrist. Vivian's interruption enhanced Rosie's rage. Once we were out of her room, she ripped the wifi unit out of the wall. When that didn't cause the reaction she had wanted, she wandered into the hall and slammed the cupboard doors shut as hard as she could.

"You are lucky I'm not your mom, Rosie! I would beat your ass!" Vivian screamed.

"I don't know what to do, Vivian."

"Record it."

She was right. I pulled out my phone and took a video. The camera didn't slow Rosie down; it provoked her. She ran up to me, shoved me into the couch and tried to rip my cell out of my hand.

"Get off your mom!" Vivian roared, as she bolted up to chased her to her room. Rosie let out a bloodcurdling scream. Vivian didn't touch Rosie, but the act alone scared her enough to get her back into her bedroom. She continued her fit until wearing herself out enough to fall asleep.

The next morning, I received a phone call from child protective services wanting to investigate. I wasn't surprised.

CHAPTER 39

Having a child abuse case opened by the state was the end for us. Job or no job, Vivian couldn't reside in our home. She finished gathering her belongings, and I helped her load them into the trunk of my car. We headed to a storage facility with almost everything she owned. All she was keeping on her was what would fit in a duffle bag. "This isn't what I wanted for us, Vivian. But at this point I don't have a choice. I could lose Rosie."

"I would never let that happen! I tell you all the time, you are a good mom. No matter how bad we argue, I've always stood up for you."

"You can't be here when Child Protective Services arrives." My eyes were watering as I struggled to hold back my tears.

"My friend can't grab me tonight until about 8:00 pm."

"That's fine, just go for a walk or something before they arrive. You can come back after and wait. I'm not trying to kick you out, I hope you know that, but it's my obligation as a parent to protect Rosie and this conflict has to end."

After the short drive to the storage facility we unloaded Vivian's belongings. We had just pulled back into my apartment complex when her phone rang. "Hello," she answered. "Yes. This is Vivian." I couldn't make out what was being said on the other end of the line. "Uh, huh. Yes! I'm still interested." I knew where it was going. "Absolutely! When? Three weeks? Sounds great! Thank you!" It was the break she had been waiting for. She hung up the phone and gave me an enormous smile.

"That was the amusement park in Iowa! I got the job I was hoping for, it's a management position. They even have employee housing. I leave in three weeks!" I didn't know she had been looking for work out of state.

There was no holding back my emotions any longer. I was sobbing like a baby. I had tears of delight for my partner and her long awaited break, but also tears of grief for the end of our relationship.

I still had to get my ass to work and deal with the CPS worker after. I let Vivian out of the car, she gave me a quick hug and mouthed, "I'll message you later." She was already back on her phone spreading the news. I had pulled myself together by the time I arrived to my job.

That evening, I received a call from our case manager letting me know she was on her way. I shoved Vivian's bag into a closet as she readied for her walk. She opened the door, and we both discovered it was raining. "You can take my umbrella," I offered. She declined, "I'll be fine."

Ten minutes later there was a knock on my door. I turned the handle and greeted a small woman holding a clipboard. "Do you know why I'm here?" she asked, taking a seat on my sofa.

"I have an idea, and to be honest, I'm not surprised." I explained what had been going on with Rosie; her coming out as transgender and the recent outbursts. I even played her the video.

"One accusation was about mom's boyfriend threatening a child, saying he would 'kick her ass.'" She gave me a worried expression when I chuckled.

"I don't have a boyfriend, I have a transgender girlfriend," I pointed out. Lucky for us the woman seemed empathetic. I explained that Vivian was no longer living with us and planning to move to Iowa. "It's like living with a testosterone raged 11-year-old boy, and an estrogen pumped 12-year-old girl, all they do is fight." She laughed as she jotted down notes. It was a good thing she had a sense of humor. She pulled Rosie aside and asked her a series of questions.

When she was through, she concluded her visit, "I'll close this case since Vivian seems to be the main issue, and she won't be living here any longer. It sounds to me like it's resolved itself."

After she left, I sent Vivian a text telling her she could return home. She arrived soaked and shivering. She rinsed off and changed while I put her wet clothes into a plastic bag.

Rosie was ecstatic, she was about to be rid of her arch enemy for good. She went to sleep without a fight, but sneaked in a "fuck you" to Vivian with her middle finger on her way to bed. Once she closed her door, I pulled out two half consumed growlers from the fridge. "We might as well finish these off," I said, pouring each of us a frosted mug full.

I was crying again. Damn it!

"Aww, Five. You are gonna miss me, huh?"

"You have no idea. I love you. You are my best friend."

"Aww, don't worry. I'll always be your friend."

I opened my wallet and handed her a $20 bill. "You can't go without a little cash."

Before we finished our drinks, Vivian received a text that her ride was waiting for her downstairs. She took me into her arms and squeezed me tight. "Stay cool Five. I love you, girl." I watched as she picked up her duffle bag and headed out my door for the last time.

EPILOUGE

V ivian was out of our lives for good, and I was back to giving Rosie my full attention. I scheduled her appointments with the counselor and the endocrinologist. She needed her hormones checked again. A week after they tested her blood we received the results. Rosie was not yet in puberty. The doctors chalked her behavior up to her age and told me it was just something we would have to experience.

Having Vivian out of our lives didn't seem to help Rosie's attitude. Her tantrums became a regular occurrence. She wasn't only acting up at home, but also in school. Like the year before, I was spending far too much time in the principal's office.

One morning, after refusing to go to class, I called the truancy officer. He picked up Rosie, led her to the back of his car, and drove her to school. Though it had been a hard thing to do, I knew she needed to learn a lesson.

"Hello, Ms. Five," the principal greeted me over the phone an hour after she had gone. "I had a long talk with Rosie about the importance of an education. You sure lucked out with the officer who brought her here today. He helped lecture her. We both assured Rosie school wasn't an option but a legal requirement. I'm hoping things will change for the better."

"Are you going to go to school on your own now?" I asked my child after she returned home that day. "I heard you had a long talk with the policeman and principal." Rosie shrugged. "I don't care! They didn't scare me!"

The following morning, I was startled awake. It was a black shadow looming over me. I almost screamed before I realized it was Rosie. Her eyes were dark and her expression resembled something out of a horror movie. "What?" I asked.

"I missed my bus."

"Get dressed! I'll drive you!" She stomped her feet on the way to the bedroom, then bashed the walls before putting on her clothes. Once in the car, she pounded my dashboard with her fists. "Rosie! If you don't stop this behavior, I will ground you from your phone for the rest of the week!" I pulled up to the school, and she climbed out.

BOOM!

She slammed the door so hard; I thought it would snap off. I finally understood what Vivian had been talking about. On my way home I called her and gave her the "run down."

"I told you that bitch rages! You blamed me for everything she did, but you never realized what she was like when you weren't around."

"I get it... I miss you, girl."

"When are you gonna come visit, Five?"

"As soon as you buy me a plane ticket."

"I can't right now, I'm saving for a car."

"Then I guess I'll wait. Anyway, you fucking owe me for the DUI. It cost about $10,000."

"That was your own fault, you shouldn't have hit me!" she said.

We both fell silent. I changed the subject.

"I had a dream I was making out with you last night."

"Oh yeah? Was it hot?" she asked.

"Fuck yeah, it was hot!"

"I wanna fuck you, girl!" she said.

"Really? I thought you were dead down there?"

"You don't know what I can do to you yet. We were barely together a year and most of that there was a kid around."

I was getting wet. "I wanna suck on you until you burst and then drink it."

"Asterisk, you are so hot when you want to be!"

"Only for you, baby. You'll always get me horny, even after you have a pussy. **But next time I get two fingers.**"

Cut snip cut

Snip Snip Snip, Once i was home alone and i was 11 years old i was in 5th grade and i was not chipper. First i was home alone i decided to cut my hair nobody new intele i told my mom she told all of her friends and i did not like that.

I did not want to brush my hair because it hurts to brush my hair. My hair gets tangled up sometimes when i dont brush it. I cut my hair because it takes a long time to brush my hair so that day i cut it. I was not happy though.

Next i told my mom that i cut my hair and i did not like telling her. "I cut my hair." I was scared to tell her that i cut my hair. it was a disaster then i told her that i cut my hair. I was scared that i did cut my hair.

When my mom knew she was nutty real nutty than she told my great grandma romate and more friends. I did not like when she told all of her friends. I got nutty to and i was real nutty to.She told everyone that i cut my hair.

Lastly Then i said sorry and my mom but my mom was batty but she forgave me and than we were merry. My mom was still a little daft at me but later she was jolly. I was relieved that that we were up. Than she forgave me and still to this day she shows everybody my hair spot that i cut off.I am not really blest that my mom tells people that spot still to this day she tells them about it.

ABOUT THE AUTHOR

Wendi Bear began her writing career in 2012 blogging, "It's not my fault" at Electrikkiss.com

Inspired by the blog, her first novel, "It's not my fault. Self Discovery & Admission," published in 2013

Her second full-length novel, "It's not my fault. Sacrifice & Survival," and "It's not my fault. MICROBOOK (One)," published in 2014

"Death & Denial, A Novelette," published in 2014

All books are available through Amazon and Kindle Unlimited.

You can follow Wendi Bear online at:

Electrikkiss.com

Facebook.com/Electrikkiss

Instagram@Electrikkiss

Twitter@Electrikkiss

Made in the USA
San Bernardino, CA
30 July 2019